FOLLOW THE CRUMBS

A COZY QUILTS CLUB MYSTERY

BOOK ONE

MARSHA DEFILIPPO

FREE BONUS MATERIAL

Receive your free copy of the Preview to *A Cozy Quilts Club Mystery series.*

Click here

To get the latest information on new releases, excerpts and more, be sure to sign up for Marsha's newsletter.

https://marshadefilippo.com/newsletter

PROLOGUE

*S*adie Emerson, 83 years old, hard of hearing, and with limited night vision even in the best of circumstances, peered out into the moonless night from her back door which opened onto her expansive back yard and the thicket of woods which marked its border. Her dog, a Jack Russell terrier named Boscoe, was standing just beyond the edge where the illumination from the house's motion light ended and darkness began, barking at something out of Sadie's line of sight. He was facing her neighbor's front porch, which was set back farther from the main road than Sadie's.

"Boscoe, come back in here," Sadie called. She couldn't see whatever it was Boscoe was barking at but wanted him back in sooner than later in case it was a porcupine. The last thing she needed was an emergency trip to the vet at nine o'clock at night. "Come on. Leave whatever it is you think you see alone and get back in here," she called again when he didn't respond.

Boscoe gave one more bark to get in the last word before turning and running back into the house and Sadie shut the door behind him.

"What did you see, Boscoe?" she asked and gave him a pat

on the head and scratched behind his ears in the way people do, even knowing there will be no response they can understand.

Boscoe whined, trying his best to communicate.

"Time to go to bed," Sadie said, making sure the door was locked before turning out the kitchen light and walking down the hallway toward her bedroom. She was about to enter the room when she heard a knock on her front door. Boscoe began to growl low in his throat and the fur on his back rose, making Sadie anxious as well. She considered ignoring the knock, hoping whoever it was would assume she was in bed and go away, but it began again.

"Come on, boy, let's go see who this is."

The motion light had already turned on and when she drew the curtain aside in the living room window, it offered a view of her front door. She relaxed when she recognized the man standing on her porch.

"It's okay, Boscoe," she said, shushing the dog and turning on the overhead light before opening the door and stepping aside to let her visitor inside. "I'm so sorry. Did Boscoe's barking disturb you? I think he might have spotted a porcupine and I was trying to bring him back inside," she was offering as explanation and apology when she saw her visitor raising his hand. It looked like he had something in it and was going to strike her with it.

Confused, she had remained standing near the door.

"No, no…" she pleaded when the realization of what was happening dawned on her, and she was helpless to prevent it. The fatal blow landed on her head, and she fell to the floor. Boscoe leaped over her body to attack the intruder, his teeth sinking into the man's arm but let loose when he received a blow to his head, just as had happened to his owner.

CHAPTER ONE

*E*va Perkins was enjoying retirement, but the luxury of having so much free time on her hands had turned into boredom after two months. She had been an elementary school teacher in a neighboring town for thirty-five years and was finding retirement was a double-edged sword of having the freedom of time on one side and missing the energy of her students on the other. She'd considered volunteering in her local community as a way to fill her time, but a spur-of-the-moment stop at her local quilt shop led to signing up for a free-motion quilting class and a new passion for life. Although she'd dabbled at making quilts over the years, she'd never taken a formal class and thought it might improve her skills as well as introduce her to some fresh faces. The four students in the class had gotten along so well they'd formed their own quilt club and she was hosting the first meeting.

She'd given the house one last cleaning touch up and baked a batch of oatmeal raisin cookies to serve for dessert along with the Niçoise salad she'd made for the potluck dinner. The fragrance of freshly baked cookies lingered in the air, adding another layer of comfort to her cape-style home where she lived alone following her divorce, with only her Maine coon cat, Reuben, to keep her company. The cat was better company than her ex-husband ever was, in Eva's opinion. Both she and her ex had married later in life, too late to consider becoming parents, so she had no children of her own. Her students had been her surrogate children. When she was honest with herself, Eva acknowledged her ex wasn't the only one to blame for their divorce. After having lived on their own for so many years and both being independent individuals, they weren't able to transition to sharing their living space and had mutually agreed to go their separate ways. Since Eva had owned her home before their marriage, she'd been the one to continue living there once they split. She hadn't thought she'd ever be in another romantic relationship, but she'd changed her mind after being introduced to Jim Davis. They'd met at the party of a mutual friend two years ago. He was a retired state policeman who also lived in her rural town of Glen Lake. He had been widowed for four years and had two grown children, Jacob and Stephanie, and three grandchildren ranging in ages from four to ten. They had hit it off almost immediately and were still going strong. Not wanting to repeat her last breakup and knowing she preferred living on her own, she had made it clear early on in their dating the one non-negotiable was maintaining separate residences. She was relieved to find Jim felt the same way. They might renegotiate that at some time in the future, but for now, it worked.

A few years before she retired, she had converted half of the two-car garage into a large sewing studio. The bookcases covering one wall were filled with fabric and quilting books she'd accumulated over the years, and an eight foot by four-foot table she'd built herself provided plenty of room for cutting material and assembling quilts. She even had room for a kitchen table and chairs to would provide seating space for the meeting.

What's all this about? Reuben's voice sounded in her head. Something Eva didn't share with others, including those who were close to her, was her ability to communicate telepathically with most animals. She had been able to do it her entire life and when she was a young girl, she'd thought all people had that ability. Being told it was just her imagination by adults and teased by other schoolchildren had taught her to hide her ability, though.

"I've invited some ladies over to start a quilting club. You mind your manners," Eve warned him.

You know only you can hear me, Reuben replied, narrowing his eyes to show his disdain for her warning.

"I do," Eva said, "which is why I've asked you to mind your manners, since you know I can't acknowledge your comments."

Reuben had been sitting on the floor looking up at Eva but instead of saying more, he stood up and stretched before turning his back on her and walking into the living room. He jumped up to the bay window and lay down on his favorite cushion, tucking his front paws together in front of him to resume surveying his domain.

There's a car pulling in, he announced.

"Thanks! The rest of the ladies should be arriving soon. Remember…"

I got it. Mind my manners.

Eva restrained herself from adding anything more. She gave one last look around in case something was out of place which she'd forgotten earlier but found everything satisfactory as her doorbell rang.

Annalise Jordan was the first to arrive. She was the closest to Eva's age but a 180-degree difference in personality and style, which leaned heavily toward Bohemian, and today was no exception. She arrived wearing a bright green paisley print, knee-length full skirt with a ruffle on the hem and an orange V-neck tee-shirt top accessorized with a long pale green silk scarf draped around her neck twice, leaving the tails hanging in front. Each of her fingers was adorned with at least one ring and both arms had several bracelets, and in her ears, she wore earrings cascading nearly to her shoulders. Today she had a green gem stud in her nose piercing.

Where's her tattoos? Eva heard Reuben's snarky question. She chose to dispense with a verbal response but gave him a seething warning glance instead.

"Annalise, welcome! I hope you found me okay?" Eva asked as she let her in.

"No problem at all. Your directions were perfect. I brought a Farro salad for the potluck. It should be refrigerated unless we're eating right away." She had a large, covered glass bowl in her hands, along with a tote bag and her purse.

"Let me take this for you," Eva offered, holding out her hands to retrieve the dish. "Can I offer you something to drink?"

"A glass of water would be good and if you have a slice of lemon, that would be wonderful."

With Annalise following behind, Eva walked toward the kitchen but only made it as far as the dining room. The sound of the doorbell ringing made them both turn toward the front door.

Eva set the bowl down on the dining room table to answer the door, turning over her shoulder to address Annalise as she walked in that direction. "I might as well wait until I let whoever this is in, and we can all go to the kitchen together."

Both Sarah Pascal and Jennifer Ryder had arrived at the same time. Sarah lived in nearby Bangor and Eva, Annalise, and Jennifer lived in Glen Lake.

"Come in, come in," Eva said. "I'm so glad you made it. Annalise is already here. Follow me and we can put the food in the kitchen before going out to my studio so we can chat for a few minutes first." She became aware of Reuben's gaze on her as he sat in the middle of the entrance to the living room on her left. "I should have thought of this earlier, but is anyone allergic to cats? If so, I can put Reuben in one of the upstairs bedrooms until it's time for everyone to leave."

She felt his indignation radiating from his body without having to look in his direction when he uttered, *Don't you dare even think about it!*

Annalise looked from Reuben to Eva, one eyebrow slightly raised, but she kept whatever she was thinking to herself.

"Oh, he is gorgeous!" Jennifer cooed. "He's a Maine coon cat, isn't he? And no, I'm not allergic."

"Me either," Annalise and Sarah both replied.

"You've gotten a reprieve, Reuben. No need to banish you to the upstairs," Eva told him.

As if you could! he said, before standing up and sauntering to the bay window and his cushion, as if to punctuate she was not the boss of him.

Chuckling to herself as she knew exactly what he was doing, Eva turned leading the way through the formal dining room and continuing into the large kitchen. A recent remodel had brought it up to modern design aesthetics with dark blue lower cabinets and white uppers and white quartz countertops on the cabinets and the island with room to seat two people. The window above the farm style sink on the back wall looked out onto the expansive gardens which Eva had designed and tended as her serenity space as well as providing fresh vegetables and herbs.

The various dishes for the potluck supper safely stored in the refrigerator and drinks served, the three women followed Eva through the large case opening between the kitchen and dining room area leading to her sewing studio.

Four six-foot-tall bookcases were set against one wall, one of which held her collection of quilting books and cloth bins she had made in a variety of colors into which she had stored scraps from projects she'd been working on in the corresponding colors. In the other three bookcases was her stash of material, also sorted by color.

"What did you use to wrap the fabric around?" Jennifer asked.

"Instead of comic book backing boards like some organizers suggest, I used magazine backing boards because they're a little bigger. They're eight and a half by eleven inches, which makes them a lot easier to fold fabric around. I lay the pieces out lengthwise, fold it in quarters, and then wrap it around the backing board so it will stand upright. It works perfectly for forty-four-inch-wide fabrics."

"I love how it all looks. It's almost like going into a quilt store," Annalise said.

"This cutting table is fantastic," Sarah said.

"I made it myself," Eva told them. "I designed it to be four feet by eight feet so I could use a standard size of melamine. Making this was how I learned to do pocket holes."

"I'm impressed," Jennifer said.

"Your sewing machine station looks so functional. The extension on the back and having your machine set down into the top so it's level must come in so handy when you're doing your free motion quilting. I might steal your idea of putting your different presser feet still in their packaging on the pegboard right beside your machine when I buy new ones," Annalise said.

"It does make it so much easier to have them within arm's reach," Eva agreed. "My blue-sky dream is to have a long arm quilting machine. Maybe someday."

"You even have the extra wide ironing board! And is that one of those Oliso irons that pops up on its own, so you don't have to worry about leaving your iron down and burning your ironing board cover?" Sarah asked.

"I made the top myself and then put it over my old ironing board. It was surprisingly easy, and I'd be happy to give you the directions if any of you would like to make one for yourself. It makes it so much easier to iron quilt tops and lengths of fabric. And, yes, it is an Oliso. I love the convenience of having it pop up when it's in the horizontal position, but I have to remind myself when I use a regular iron to put it upright."

"Did you put the table and chairs in for us?" Jennifer asked.

"No, it was already here. It's serendipity that it will work out perfectly for our meeting."

"Eva, I'm so jealous!" Jennifer told her after taking it all in.

"Me, too!" Sarah said. "Ashley would never let me convert the garage, but there's no extra space in our house to dedicate as a sewing room. I'd love to have a spot where I could leave my projects out instead of having to clean up every time I'm done for the day. She doesn't do well with clutter."

"I know what you mean," Jennifer said with a smile. "David is the same way and with the winters we have, there's no way he'd let me convert even half of the garage."

"I don't know about you ladies, but I'm starving. How about we head back to the kitchen and eat dinner?" Eva asked.

"I'll second that," Sarah said.

"It occurred to me too late leaving the potluck part to chance might not have been the best idea," Eva said as she retrieved the various dishes from the refrigerator. "If you've had the same experience as I have, we might all have thought of either the same thing or nothing goes together. Maybe next time we can have a theme or put the courses in a hat and draw names for who brings what and then rotate going forward. I also totally forgot to ask if anyone needed to have their dish placed in the oven instead of in the microwave," but everyone shook their head.

"I like your idea about switching up the courses," Jennifer agreed. "I'd be okay with that, and it would take some of the pressure off for what to bring if I knew what course I should be making. We can work around everyone's schedules, too. For tonight, though, I'll eat anything about now. I didn't have lunch and my stomach is not in a forgiving mood," which made everyone laugh.

"I'm a little embarrassed I didn't actually cook anything," Sarah apologized. "I lost track of the days because I've been so busy with work, and it wasn't until I saw the event on my calendar I was reminded our meeting was today. I cheated and went to the Whoopie Pie Factory. I bought an assortment since I wasn't sure what anyone might like. I thought if we cut them in half or even quarters, we can each sample as many as we'd like. If I could borrow a plate, I'll cut them up and they'll have time to come to room temperature while we eat."

Eva handed her a plate and a knife and a box of plastic wrap to cover them once they were cut and arranged.

"You don't have to apologize as far as I'm concerned," Annalise said. "My sweet tooth is very happy. You have two of my favorite kinds, carrot cake and red velvet. What's the filling in this blueberry one?" she asked.

"It's lemon. I like cream cheese fillings better for Whoopie pies myself, but the combination of blueberry and lemon sounded good."

"I think I may have drooled on myself," Eva joked. "Before we get to dessert, though, I decided to make a Niçoise Salad but with shrimp instead of tuna, so not the traditional recipe. I thought it would be easier to divide with the shrimp, but to be honest, it had more to do with the fact I prefer shrimp over tuna."

Uncovering her dish, Annalise described its contents. "I made my version of a Mediterranean Farro Salad. If you haven't ever had farro before, it's a grain similar to brown rice and it does have gluten in case you are avoiding that. It has a slightly nutty taste. The salad has grape tomatoes, cucumbers, roasted red peppers, black olives, red onion, feta cheese and a vinaigrette dressing. I have a Persian lime infused olive oil which I mixed with red wine vinegar, a quarter teaspoon of oregano, a pinch of garlic powder, and salt and pepper. Oh, and some parsley tossed in."

"It's so pretty. I can't wait to try it," Jennifer said. "You all made such interesting dishes. I'm feeling a little plain and ordinary as I stuck to the old standby of a pasta salad."

"It's all good and I mean that in the culinary as well as the figurative sense of the phrase, so don't feel like you have to apologize, Jennifer," Eva reassured her.

"I agree, let's dig in," Sarah said, picking up a plate and scooping out a serving of the pasta salad before moving on to the other dishes.

Once they'd finished their meals, they headed back to the studio.

"This may seem a little silly since we've already met, but I thought we could use this first meeting to get to know each other a little better," Eva began. "We didn't have much time at the free motion class to do more than talk about quilting. I realize it can be awkward, so I'll start since it was my idea unless someone else would like to go first."

"I'm more than happy to let you be first," Jennifer replied, smiling.

"Well, then, my name is Eva and I'm a fabricaholic," she began, and everyone laughed, which helped to break the ice further. "I'm retired and divorced, not in that order. I married later in life, and it didn't take me long before I realized I'm not built to be around someone 24/7 for more than short amounts of time. I don't have any children, but I am *in a relationship,"* which she emphasized with air quotes, "as the saying goes these days, unless that's changed already," she looked at the two younger women who shook their heads to affirm it was still the right verbiage. "His name is Jim Davis, and he's a retired Maine State trooper. I've been quilting off and on for the past twenty years, but never had the time to commit to it while I was working full time. I think that's about it for now."

The others looked around, each waiting to see who would go next, until at last, Jennifer volunteered.

"I'm married with two teenagers. My husband's name is David. My son, Matthew, is eighteen and will be a senior this year. Nicole is sixteen and a sophomore. I work part time at my husband's insurance agency. I've been quilting for about ten years. My great-aunt, Sadie, taught me. She lives across from me on the Hudson Road and is the sweetest lady I've ever met. She's been like a mother to me since my parents live out of state and her children do, too, so I've filled in for them watching out for her."

Jennifer then turned to Sarah to indicate she was finished.

"Okay, then. I've only been quilting a couple of years. I live in Bangor with my wife, Ashley. We don't have any children yet. I work remotely from home for a security firm, but I can't say more without violating a few non-disclosure agreements. My job can be stressful at times and quilting has helped relax me, so I'm really glad to be with all of you. Too often, I let my job take over, which is easy to do when you're working from home and it's always right there if you don't have an office to commute to."

That left only Annalise. She had been sitting quietly observing the others while they made their introductions.

"I've been quilting for about the same time as Eva, but this is the first time I've ever joined a quilting club or guild. I'd taken classes before but never felt the connection to the other students the way I did with all of you. I'm a Reiki practitioner and I sometimes do Tarot card readings but that's only if a client has shown an interest after we've gotten to know each other. Ever since I was a little girl, I've had psychic abilities. It's not something I would always bring up right away, but I have a very strong sense each of you may have paranormal abilities you don't always share, either." She looked at each of the women's faces in turn. No one else offered an immediate response, but the atmosphere became charged until broken by Reuben's loud meow before jumping up into Eva's lap. Annalise looked from Reuben to Eva. "You can communicate with your cat."

Eva's eyes widened. She'd dismissed Annalise's first proclamation about paranormal abilities as being a wild guess of someone who used generalities to try to convince people they had insight into another realm, but this was too spot on.

"You can communicate with other animals, too. You've done it since you were a child, but you've hidden it from others because you were afraid of being ridiculed," Annalise went on.

Eva blinked as though waking up from a dream. "Yes, that's true," she finally answered. "How did you know?"

"I can't really explain the process, but I've had this ability my entire life as well. It comes in different ways. Sometimes I hear the messages, other times it will be images. It's not something I control. It just happens."

Sarah and Jennifer had been watching the interplay, not sure how to react to what had happened. Annalise turned to face Jennifer and closed her eyes.

"Your gift is psychometry. You're able to receive messages from or information about the person who owned an object when you hold it or perhaps by touching a person's physical body," she announced after a minute, opening her eyes again.

"Yes," Jennifer whispered. "I haven't even told my husband that."

Annalise turned to face Sarah and closed her eyes.

"You can communicate with the dead, like the boy in the movie *The Sixth Sense*."

"Whoa, how do you do that?" Sarah replied, wide-eyed.

"Like I said, it just comes to me, although rarely do I have such strong impressions as I did now. I could tell something was there but with all the distractions at the quilt class, it was too blurry to grasp."

The ladies all looked at one another and smiled; the weight of their secrets which had been heavy for so long suddenly lightened.

Should we all start singing Kumbaya?

Eva laughed despite herself, and the others looked expectantly at her to explain why or what she was laughing at.

"Reuben asked me if we should start singing Kumbaya."

They all laughed with her, and the mood was back to the normality of every day.

"It will probably be boring after what we've just been discussing, but why don't we talk about quilting," Eva said. "I have an idea I'd like to pass by you to see what you think. Unless you already know," she teased Annalise.

"Just because I'm psychic doesn't mean I know everything about what's going to happen," Annalise countered. "It's one of those contradictions people always bring up to try to dismiss it if they don't believe it's an actual ability. It's okay, I didn't take that personally," she told Eva and gave her a pat on the shoulder to reassure her she was not offended.

Eva continued with the idea she'd mentioned.

"If you ladies are anything like me, you have been saving scraps from other projects because you can't bear to throw them away."

They all nodded, sheepish expressions on their faces.

"Have you heard of crumb quilts?"

"Isn't that where you take the scraps and randomly stitch them together to make a piece of fabric you can then use to make quilt blocks?" Jennifer asked.

"Exactly! I was thinking we could use crumb quilting as a theme, but each of us can make our own project using the scraps we have. Perhaps small projects or mini quilts we would finish in about a month and then go on to another project. What do you think?"

"I love that idea!" Annalise said. "I do love to quilt blankets, but my real passion is making art quilts so I can have more freedom of expression. In case you haven't noticed, I have a bit of a Bohemian streak about me."

The woman does have a gift for understatement, Reuben drawled, and Eva gave him a look.

"I've always wanted to do a crazy quilt. This would be a

great way to do one of those," Jennifer added. "Doing a mini-quilt would be a perfect way to sample the techniques without committing to a regular quilt size."

"I might do a mug rug this time around. My workload is going to be crazy the next couple of weeks, so I probably won't have a lot of extra time to commit to something bigger," Sarah said.

"I was thinking I would do a journal cover. I bought several small notebooks over a year ago intending to make covers for them to use as gifts, but never got around to making the covers," Eva said. "It sounds like we have a plan for this next week. I'm more than happy to host next week's session here as well."

"You have such a beautiful studio, I wouldn't mind coming here every week!" Sarah said.

"Would you mind?" Jennifer asked.

"Not at all. I have a couple of folding banquet tables I can set up so everyone would have a space to put their sewing machines and supplies… Oh, wait, I forgot we don't have a name. I'd thought about the Cozy Quilts Club, but I'm open to other suggestions."

"It works for me," Annalise agreed.

"Me, too," Jennifer and Sarah said at the same time.

"Well, then, the only other thing we need to do is pick names and courses for next week's potluck. Does anyone want to suggest a theme, or should we wing it again? I'll let you think it over while I get some paper and a pen." Eva said.

They sat silently, considering options while they waited for Eva to return until Annalise piped up, "What if we each tried to find a recipe with crumbs as one of the ingredients? Maybe a crumb cake for dessert, something with bread crumbs in the main dish…?"

"Oh, that's perfect!" Eva said.

"I agree," Jennifer said, and Sarah nodded her agreement as well.

Eva took the four slips of paper she'd brought back, using one of each to write appetizer, salad, main, and dessert course, then put them into a basket and offered it first to Annalise to pick out one of the slips. After Jennifer and Sarah had picked out their slip, she took the last one.

"Okay, dinner selections are settled. Unless anyone else has anything to bring up, this first meeting of the Cozy Quilts Club is now adjourned!" Eva said and, after no one else offered any more discussion, rapped her knuckles on the table, not having a gavel to use instead.

CHAPTER TWO

*J*ennifer thought about checking on Sadie before going home, but the meeting had run longer than she expected and if Sadie had already gone to bed, she didn't want to disturb her. As she pulled into her driveway, she glanced over at Sadie's house and noticed the light on in her living room but decided to wait until morning. It wasn't unusual for Sadie to forget to turn out a light before going to bed and it was past her usual bedtime.

"How did it go?" David asked when she came into the kitchen, where he was unloading the dishwasher.

"It was fantastic! I knew they were an interesting group from what little interaction we'd had at the class, but let's just say I think I may have found my soul sisters."

David's left eyebrow raised but he wisely didn't tease her, and instead left it at, "I'm glad you've found new friends and are doing something you enjoy, not just another committee which ends up being a lot of work for little reward."

"Amen to that," Jennifer agreed. "I'm sorry we didn't spend much time together tonight, but I think I'm going to bed. I'm exhausted."

"I'll be right behind you as soon as the dishes are put away."

Jennifer gave him a kiss and went first to the bathroom to brush her teeth and then on to bed.

* * *

ONCE SHE'D CLEANED the breakfast dishes and the kids had gone to school, Jennifer decided to check on Sadie. She had awoken with an uneasy sensation and wished she had checked on her the night before.

"I'm going over to Sadie's house to check on her," she called to David but didn't wait for his response. He wouldn't be leaving for work for another twenty minutes and she would be back before he left.

As she walked up to the front stairs, she noticed the light was still on in Sadie's living room.

"That's odd. I'm surprised Sadie hasn't turned that off yet."

She knocked on the door but there was no answer. She gave Sadie a couple minutes in case she wasn't able to come to open it right away, but the premonition of something being wrong was getting stronger. Even if Sadie hadn't come soon after she heard the knock, Boscoe would usually bark regardless of whether he knew who was on the other side of the door.

"Maybe they're both in the back yard," she said, hoping to reassure herself. She used the spare key she had for emergencies or occasions like this but when she turned the key, she could tell the door had not been locked.

She opened the door to find Sadie and Boscoe beside her, both lying motionless on the floor. Boscoe whimpered but didn't lift his head to greet her. She was frozen in horror when her brain finally made sense of what she was seeing.

"Sadie! *Sadie,* are you alright?" she asked, her voice panicked.

She bent down and felt for a pulse, even though she knew

she wouldn't find one. She then went to Boscoe and patted his back, speaking to him softly.

"What happened here, buddy?"

He whimpered again and tried to raise his head but only got an inch from the floor before putting it back down again.

Jennifer was sobbing now and had to take deep breaths before she regained her composure enough to call 911.

"911. What is your emergency?"

"It's my aunt. I just found her in her house, and she has no pulse. Her dog is injured, too. I don't think this was an accident."

"What is the address, ma'am?"

Jennifer gave her the address and was told by the dispatcher an ambulance and officer had been notified and would be on their way, and Jennifer disconnected the call. Boscoe required medical attention but she didn't think an EMT would be trained to give the kind he needed. She hesitated a moment, not sure if she should leave Boscoe to get David, but although there was nothing she could do for Sadie, she didn't want to leave her. She dialed David's cell number instead and was relieved to have him answer on the first ring.

"I need you at Sadie's. Please come now."

"What's wrong Jennifer?"

"I'll explain when you get here but I need your help."

He was there in less than a minute. Jennifer had left the door open in her haste to check on Sadie and Boscoe, and David started to come in but then stopped suddenly, taking it all in just as Jennifer had.

"Is she...?"

"Yes. I've called 911 and they're sending someone but it's Boscoe I need help with. He's lost a lot of blood and he can't even keep his head up. We've got to get him to the vet. I know it's a lot to ask, but could you take him while I wait for the ambulance? He might not make it if we don't get him treated right away."

David didn't hesitate.

"Of course. I'll bring the car over right now. Is there anything we can wrap him in?"

"I'll look around for something. You get the car but make sure you aren't blocked in the driveway when the EMTs get here."

He turned and ran back to their house but before he made it back, Jennifer heard the sound of the siren announcing the ambulance's arrival and seconds later they had parked in Sadie's driveway. Two EMTs came into the house and surveyed the scene.

"Can you tell us what happened, ma'am?" one of them asked and the other one bent down to check for a pulse but shook his head to let his partner know it was too late.

"I came to check on Sadie… she's my great-aunt… and when no one answered the door, I used my key to get in. This is how I found them. I checked for a pulse first and then called 911. Boscoe needs to be taken to the vet right away. He's alive but badly hurt. My husband is coming back to take him there."

Before she could say more, a sheriff's officer came through the door.

"My name is Deputy Tremblay. What's happened here?"

By the time Jennifer had repeated what she had told the EMTs, David arrived.

"I'll need to take pictures of the scene before you take him," the deputy said.

"Alright, but please hurry. I'm afraid Boscoe won't make it if we don't get him to the vet."

Deputy Tremblay nodded his head and took out his cell phone to take pictures from several angles. "Hopefully that will be enough for the Evidence Response Team considering the circumstances. You're free to take the dog now."

Jennifer had gone to find towels while the deputy was taking the pictures and now carefully wrapped Boscoe in them. He whimpered and then snapped at her when she put the towel around his head, but she understood it was only because he was in pain. David had bent down to help and lifted Boscoe in his arms.

He gave Jennifer a kiss and whispered in her ear, "I'll be back as soon as I can. I'll close the office today so I can be with you."

"Thank you," she said, the gratitude showing in her eyes.

David left and Jennifer was told she was free to leave soon after. She had given Deputy Tremblay both her address and phone number and that of her cousin, Melissa Patterson, who was Sadie's daughter. He had given her one of his business cards and added his cell number on the back and told her he would come to her house if he needed anything more.

Still in shock and feeling numb, she went back to her house, dreading the phone call she was going to have to make to tell Melissa the heartbreaking news.

CHAPTER THREE

*E*va was going about her routine of watching the noontime news report while she ate her lunch when the name Sadie Emerson caught her attention. *Wasn't that the name of Jennifer's great-aunt?* she thought. Sadie wasn't a common name, so she paid more attention to the report of a murder the night before which had happened right in her own hometown. The anchor was reporting the victim had been found by her grandniece, Jennifer Ryder.

"Oh, no!" Eva said aloud, causing Reuben to look up from his after-breakfast grooming.

What's wrong?

"You remember Jennifer from my quilting club?"

It hasn't even been twenty-four hours since she left. I haven't developed dementia since then. She was the one with the two teenagers, Reuben replied.

"That's right. She mentioned she lives across the road from her aunt, so checks in on her. The news report said she's the one who found her aunt's body."

She's not a suspect, is she? We really don't want a homicidal maniac coming to our house, do we?

"She's not a homicidal maniac," Eva replied, her annoyance obvious. "Oh, the poor thing. I'll have to call later to see if I can do anything for her."

Eva's cell phone rang and looking at the caller ID, she saw it was Annalise.

"Hello, Annalise. Are you watching the news about Jennifer's aunt?"

"Yes, that's why I'm calling. Do you think we should cancel next week's meeting out of respect?"

"I was thinking of calling Jennifer later today to ask how she's doing and go from there."

"That makes sense. Let me know when you can. I don't want to bother her, too, but please tell her I'm thinking of her and if there's anything I can do for her, don't hesitate to ask."

"Will do. I'll talk to you later."

Eva backed up the DVR recording to listen to the portion of the report she'd missed while she was on the phone with Annalise. The anchor was saying it appeared to be a robbery gone wrong, and the police speculated it might have been motivated by drugs as they found evidence of the contents of the bathroom medicine cabinet having been disturbed but it was too early in the investigation to be certain. Eva turned off the television and sat thinking about the odds of having a murder committed in their little town of less than five thousand people and to the family of someone she knew. She hadn't known Sadie Emerson, but her work hours had kept her from socializing with many of her neighbors and she wasn't one to take part in community events so even though it was a small town, it was still possible to be a stranger.

She shook herself out of her reverie and decided to call her partner, Jim, to find out if he knew more than what was in the news. They had been dating for the past two years, but Eva still couldn't bring herself to call Jim her boyfriend. It didn't seem age appropriate. Although he was a retired Maine State trooper, he played poker every week with several other law enforcement officers, some retired and others still active duty. She'd purposely chosen the same night as his poker game to have the quilt club meeting. It was probably too soon for him to have any updates given that the murder had occurred during the same time as the game, but she found the idea of speaking to someone else comforting.

"Hello there, sunshine," Jim's chipper voice came through the line.

"Hello to you, too," Eva replied, a smile on her face, hearing his upbeat greeting. "How was the poker game?"

"I managed to not lose my shirt but can't claim to be a winner. How was the quilt meeting?"

"It went great. I think it's going to be a lot of fun." She thought briefly about sharing the revelations of each of the members having a paranormal ability, but decided it was better to keep that piece of information close to the vest for now. It would mean making a true confession of her own she wasn't ready to share. "Did you hear the news about the murder here in town last night, though? One of my group is the grandniece of the victim."

"I'm sorry to hear that. I'm aware of the report but didn't recognize the names."

"That's partly why I was calling. I wondered if any of your cop buddies had said something about it. The news is saying they think it was drug-related, but should I be worried about a killer on the loose?"

"I'd be happy to come by later to keep you company if you're nervous about being alone," Jim offered.

"Is that a subtle way of inviting yourself for a sleepover?" Eva teased.

"Apparently not so subtle," he chuckled.

"Sure, pack yourself an overnight bag and come for dinner, too. And if you can find out anything else about the murder, I'd love to hear about it."

She had been on the fence about calling Jennifer, but her conversation with Jim had helped so she decided to give it a try anyway. Chances were she wouldn't be going to work today, and the police would have finished interviewing her.

The phone was on its third ring and Eva was preparing herself to leave a voice message when Jennifer answered. It was easy to tell she had been crying and Eva almost regretted the call, fearing it was an intrusion.

"Jennifer, it's Eva. I'm so sorry if this isn't a good time to call, but I wanted to let you know how sorry I was to hear about your aunt on the noontime news and to ask you if there is anything I can do. Annalise asked me to pass along that message as well."

"That's very kind of both of you. It's so surreal. I'm still numb and haven't fully processed it's happened. I mean, who would want to hurt Sadie? She was the sweetest person and didn't deserve to die like that."

"Do the police have any idea of who might have killed her?"

"No. There weren't any obvious clues at the scene other than her medicine cabinet having been rifled, but the killer didn't leave the murder weapon. The state police crime lab is still going over the house in case they can find any prints or other evidence left to tie it to the murderer, but it will be a while before they are finished with their report. I've called my cousin and she and her husband will be arriving later today. I feel so awful. I should have checked on Aunt Sadie when I got back last night, but instead, I went straight home after our meeting. If I'd stopped instead..." her voice trailed off.

"Have they told you when she was killed? It might not have made any difference if she wasn't killed until later," Eva offered in an attempt to relieve Jennifer's guilt.

"I suppose that's possible. Even so, I can't help thinking I should have done more."

"I hope I'm not being insensitive by saying sometimes in life there's nothing we can do. Things happen which are totally out of our control. This may have been one of those things."

"Thank you for saying that. I'm sure I'll be fine. It's just so raw right now."

"That's partly why I called. If you would rather not have a meeting of the quilt club next week, I'm sure we'd all understand." Eva was about to say, "it's not a matter of life or death," but caught herself in time.

"No, please, don't cancel because of me. You should go ahead and have the meeting and if I'm up to it by then, I'll come, too. My cousin will be making all the funeral arrangements, so there's not a lot I'll need to be doing other than supporting her, and it might do me good to get out. I'll let you know either way."

"It's only a potluck dinner and your course was the appetizer, so if you are busy and don't remember to call, don't worry about it. We'll either see you then or the next week if you're able to make it. We'll all be thinking of you, and I meant it when I said to reach out to me or Annalise if there's anything we can do."

"I will. Thank you for being such a good friend."

CHAPTER FOUR

*T*he aroma of bacon and coffee was the first awareness Eva had the next morning, followed almost instantaneously by a loud growl in her stomach. She opened her eyes to find a pair of green eyes looking back at her, but they weren't Jim's. They were Reuben's.

About time you woke up.

Eva yawned and stretched.

"Didn't Jim feed you?"

He did, but you know he's not the conversationalist you are. Why is it humans think saying meow to a cat means they are talking to them? It's insulting, really. Reuben narrowed his eyes and turned his head away from Eva to emphasize his disgust.

"You realize not everyone can understand you the same way I do. We've been through this before. But even I have a hard time carrying on a conversation until I've had my coffee, and that bacon is calling my name." Eva tossed back the covers and slipped on her robe before padding out to the kitchen with Reuben trailing behind.

"Good morning! That fragrance is the best alarm clock ever!" she said.

"You timed it perfectly. I was about to come see if you were ready to get up," Jim said, giving her a quick kiss on the cheek. "I'm afraid the eggs ended up scrambled instead of over easy. Hope you don't mind."

"Not at all. I appreciate you did the cooking," she said.

They ate their breakfast in companionable silence before Eva broached what had been on her mind ever since she woke up.

"Have you found out anything from your poker buddies about the Sadie Emerson murder? We didn't talk about it last night."

"I didn't want to bring it up until you did, but they didn't have much to share yesterday that wasn't already on the news. They're thinking Sadie might have known the killer since there was no sign of forced entry. She might have caught them in the act of going through her medicine cabinet looking for prescription pain killers and the killer panicked. She has a grandson in the area who's had some addiction problems. It's difficult to think he might have killed his own grandmother to steal drugs, but it wouldn't be the first time. He's their first person of interest until they find any clues to lead them in a different direction."

"Oh, I hope not for the family's sake. It's bad enough to lose Sadie in such a violent way, but to have the killer be another family member would be devastating. I spoke to Jennifer..., the one I mentioned yesterday who is Sadie's grandniece and part of the quilting club. She's the person who found Sadie's body," Eva offered as explanation, "and she's blaming herself for not having checked on Sadie instead of going straight home. She thinks she might have been able to prevent this from happening if she'd been with Sadie and if it was another family member, she might be even more convinced she could have prevented it."

"Sometimes these things happen and there's nothing anyone could have done."

"That's exactly what I told her, but I guess it's human nature to blame yourself."

Eva cleared the dishes and placed them in the dishwasher and Jim excused himself to shower and change before heading out for the day. She was finishing up when her phone rang.

"Good morning, Annalise. How are you today?"

"I'm fine. I had a feeling you might have some news about Jennifer's aunt."

"How did...." Eva was about to ask, and then remembered Annalise had psychic abilities. She didn't always believe in such things, but then, who was she to judge when most people would think she was crazy for talking to animals. "Well, I do have it on reliable authority the police think the killer might have been someone Sadie knew since there was no forced entry. I'm not sure if they've announced this as I haven't watched the news this morning, but it's possible it was her grandson because of the drug connection and he's had addiction problems. They're considering him a person of interest."

"That's certainly a possibility, but it's not resonating for me. I think it will end up as a dead end. Did you have a chance to speak to Jennifer?"

"I did. She's very upset, as would be expected, but she thought we should go ahead and have next week's get-together as planned and if she's feeling up to it, she'll join us. Her cousin, who is Sadie's daughter, was arriving yesterday and will be handling all the funeral arrangements once the body is released. I'm hoping I was able to convince Jennifer she wasn't to blame for Sadie's death because she didn't check on her before going home. It did sound like she felt better once I'd told her it was out of her control."

"Even I didn't pick up on something about to happen I could have warned her about. Just because someone has psychic abilities doesn't mean they are all-knowing, which is a common jab non-believers like to make when they don't understand how it works. It does make it more difficult to be taken seriously, even when someone does have the gift."

"I totally understand. Well, I should be going. I hear Jim finishing up and getting ready to leave, so should say goodbye, and I want to get started on my crumb quilt piecing. I'll be sure to be in touch if I hear any updates."

Eva walked into the front entry where Jim was putting on his jacket and had his overnight bag by the door.

"I'll give you a call if there's any news… that I can share," Jim added. They both knew he would not be able to pass along any part of the investigation the police withheld from the public to prevent the killer from being alerted before they were ready to make an arrest. A tinge of guilt came over Eva as his caution reminded her she had told Annalise about Sadie's grandson being a person of interest. She'd have to be more careful about what she said going forward but chances were the information would be out to the public soon enough.

"Much appreciated. I'll be here all day. The itch to do some quilting needs scratching, so I'll be in my studio, but my cell phone will be handy. Use that number if you call or you can text me, too."

They exchanged a kiss, and Eva shut the door behind him, excited to get started on her crumb quilt project. For the next few hours, she was lost in the magic of sewing together small scraps of fabric saved from other projects. She had sorted them all out by colors into plastic bins and was randomly choosing pieces from each to sew together until she had larger pieces which she then cut into blocks. This was a habit she'd formed over the years. Whenever she had leftover fabric in large enough pieces from the project she was working on, she would cut them into 10-inch squares and add them to her stash, making her own layer cakes. This is the term quilters use to describe a collection of forty-two pre-cut ten-inch squares, usually from a similar color family or patterns. She was pleased with her morning's efforts, seeing she would have enough to not only make the journal cover for the quilting group project, but she now had several more to her growing stash of ten-inch squares. More ideas for how to use them in other projects were swirling through her head, and she grabbed the idea journal she kept in her bookcase to write them down for future reference.

Are you finally done playing?

"I'm done for now. Are you feeling ignored?" Eva asked.

Reuben lifted one paw and began licking it, ignoring her question, but Eva knew this was his way of making it known he was punishing her for having been wrapped up for so long without giving him so much as a chin scratch. She chuckled and walked back into the kitchen to make a light lunch and pour herself a drink before turning on the television to watch the noontime news report. Reuben had waited a minute before following her to make sure she didn't think he actually missed her company.

The lead story was a follow up on Sadie Emerson's murder investigation. The anchor confirmed Jim's information that a person of interest, who Eva assumed was Sadie's grandson, was being interviewed in connection with the murder, but there were no additional details. Eva considered calling Jennifer, but decided against it. If Jennifer came to the next meeting, she could offer her support then. Their friendship was too new to insert herself and it was likely Jennifer was busy in any case with other family matters. What she realized she could do, though, was make a casserole to take to her in the time-honored tradition of how neighbors helped neighbors in times like these. A plan in place, she went to her pantry to see what she had on hand.

CHAPTER FIVE

*W*ith chicken noodle casserole in hand, Eva arrived at Jennifer's house later that afternoon. Luckily, they had all exchanged addresses and phone numbers at the last meeting, so she'd known where to go. The only car in the driveway had Massachusetts license plates, which she assumed must be Jennifer's cousin. Taking a deep breath to settle her nerves, Eva rang the doorbell and was relieved when it was Jennifer who came to the door.

"Eva, how nice to see you," Jennifer said.

Her face showed the strain of her emotions and Eva almost regretted her decision, but it was too late now.

"I brought a casserole. Hopefully, you aren't already inundated with them, but it can be frozen if you want to save it for later. I don't want to intrude, as I know your cousin is here," she said and looked back at the car in the driveway. "but how are you all holding up?"

Jennifer glanced back inside before stepping out and pulling the door behind her.

"My cousin is a mess. Losing Sadie was bad enough, but now the police have questioned her son as being a possible person of interest. They found Sadie's cell phone, and he had texted that same night asking her for money, but she had told him no. They're going on the theory he might have become upset and gone to Sadie's house to try to take the money anyway. Since he's had addiction problems in the past and got into some trouble when he was a teenager which ended up in his having to do time in a juvenile detention facility, along with her medicine cabinet having been disturbed, it adds to the possibility it was him. I don't believe it, though," she said with conviction. "Thomas has had problems in the past. There's no argument about that, but he's gone to rehab and worked hard to get himself straight. And he loved Sadie. There's no way he would have hurt her, even if he has relapsed. Which I don't believe for a minute. I'd met him for lunch last week and I didn't pick up any signs he's back on drugs. It seemed like he's finally got his life on track."

Jennifer's sincerity and the conviction in her voice left no doubt in Eva's mind Annalise's intuition about the grandson not being the killer would be proven right. She reached out with one hand, balancing the casserole in the other, to stroke Jennifer's arm in reassurance.

"I believe you. It sounds like the police are doing their job following up on any leads they have, but if he has an alibi, they will have to look elsewhere. Which they may be doing in any case," she added as an afterthought.

"It might be a problem if they can't find any evidence of someone else being at Sadie's, or if he doesn't have an alibi. I'm not sure about that. If he does, Melissa… she's his mother… hasn't mentioned it. She may not know either. We haven't talked about it much other than my telling her I don't believe he is Sadie's killer."

"Hopefully, the police will be able to find something or someone else they can focus on so you can all let this be put behind you. It's already hard enough on your family," she said with what she hoped would soon turn out to be true. "Well, I should let you go back to your family. If you need someone to talk to, don't hesitate to give me a call and when you're ready to come back to the meetings, we'll be happy to have you back," she said and handed the casserole to Jennifer.

"Thank you so much, Eva. You're a good friend," Jennifer said and gave Eva a peck on the cheek.

Eva was glad she'd decided to bring the casserole. *Sometimes you have to trust your intuition*, she told herself as she got in her car to return home.

CHAPTER SIX

*A*fter the initial reports with no new leads, the local news stations had moved on to other stories by the time the Club had its next meeting. It surprised everyone Jennifer showed up.

"I'm so glad you came, Jennifer," Annalise told her.

"Me, too," Sarah agreed.

"How about a group hug?" Eva asked, holding out her arms. Everyone laughed and joined in. "Let's take a seat in the dining room and chat before we have our dinner."

Jennifer wiped a tear with the back of her hand. "You guys are the best. Thank you all for bringing casseroles. We haven't had to cook all week long with all the neighbors bringing us meals. It was very appreciated to have such an outpouring of generosity. Sadie was loved by so many people in the community. I almost didn't come tonight because I was afraid it might be rude, but I needed to get out of the house," she explained. "My cousin is still here and beside herself the police are considering her son as a person of interest. It's true Thomas has a history of drug abuse and served jail time as a juvenile for a burglary involving drugs, but he loved Sadie, and he's gotten clean."

"Are the police still looking for other suspects?" Sarah asked.

"They say they are, but it seems like they're focusing on Thomas instead. They found texts on Sadie's phone from that night. Thomas had asked to borrow money and Sadie had refused. I think she was afraid he would use it to buy drugs because it hasn't been long since he's given them up. They're trying to make it sound like Thomas got angry and came to Sadie's house to bully her into giving him the money and then things got out of hand. Thomas's side of the story is that he was going to be a little short to pay his rent and had intended it to be a loan, not a gift. I can only guess Sadie didn't want to risk it because Thomas had lied to her in the past and used the money she'd given him for drugs."

"Does he have an alibi for where he was when the murder occurred?" Eva asked. She'd known most of what Jennifer had told the group but didn't let on since it was new information to the others.

"No. He was at home by himself and no one can back him up."

Annalise had been sitting quietly while the others were talking this over. "I'm getting an impression he's telling the truth. They have the wrong person."

"Unfortunately, they'll need something more concrete than a feeling," Eva said. "No offense intended," she added, realizing her remark might have come across as dismissive.

"None taken," Annalise smiled.

"What else can we do?" Jennifer asked.

They all sat silently, considering possible options, but none came. After a few minutes, Eva broke the silence.

"Well, perhaps something will come to us later. I think if we find a way to use our special abilities, we might be able to crack this case. For now, though, let's get back to a more pleasant topic —quilting."

"I second that," Jennifer agreed. "I need a break from all the sadness, even if it's only for a couple hours and I'm ready to do some quilting."

"Should we have our dinner first, though?" Eva asked. "I'm curious about the recipes everyone found with crumbs in them."

"Why don't I start since I made the appetizer?" Jennifer asked and continued when everyone gave their nod of approval. "I made stuffed mushrooms with bread crumbs, garlic and Pecorino Romano cheese. They'll need to be warmed, but if you have a toaster oven, it should only take about five to ten minutes."

"I do! I'll get them started right now," Eva said.

"I guess I'm next since I'm the salad course," Sarah began when Eva returned from the kitchen. "It's a simple tossed salad and it may be cheating since they're not technically crumbs, but I made my own garlic croutons. I put the dressing in a separate container instead of on the salad in case anyone doesn't like vinaigrette. Plus, it would have gotten soggy by now."

"As far as I'm concerned, croutons are not cheating," Eva reassured her. "You must be next, Annalise, because I had dessert."

"Of course, the first thing I thought of was macaroni and cheese, but I wanted to take things up a notch, so I made an Eggplant Parmesan casserole. It's basically the same bread crumb topping but not mac and cheese filling, obviously. The eggplant is baked instead of fried, so lighter on calories. It should still be warm in the insulated carrier I brought it in, but if not, it can be heated in the oven or microwave."

"That leaves me. My rhubarb needed trimming, so I made a Rhubarb Bread Crumb cake and whipped cream for the topping. And I think I heard the toaster oven ding, so that's our cue to get this party started."

At the end of their meal, Sarah let out a groan as she pushed away her empty dessert plate. "I'm not sure I'll be able to move to walk into the sewing room. That was one of the best potluck dinners I've ever had. It was a great idea to draw names for the courses. It was more like a planned dinner than a potluck."

"I think I'm with you on not being able to move… and how the dinner turned out," Annalise agreed.

"How about we take a quick walk in my garden to work off some of these calories?"

"Great idea!" Jennifer said. "Let's clean up first and then take the walk."

"Your gardens are beautiful, Eva," Sarah said after they'd had their tour. "I'd love to have you give Ashley and me some ideas for what to do with our yard. It's a barren wasteland at the moment."

"I'd be happy to. Are you busy on Saturday? I could come take a look and give you some suggestions."

"That would be fantastic!"

"It's a date. Now, let's go back inside to work on our projects."

* * *

EVERYONE HAD BROUGHT their sewing machines to work on their projects and Eva had set up the room earlier in the day to give them a space for sewing. The room was soon buzzing with the sounds of sewing machines and the colorful scraps of fabric beside each workstation turned into larger pieces of fabric.

"I could keep going on this for hours! It's addictive," Annalise exclaimed when the two hours were up, and they stopped to compare their progress. "I had no idea how relaxing it is to do this type of quilting and I'm feeling very virtuous I'm not sending these little scraps to a landfill."

"I keep an old pillowcase I don't want to use anymore for all the little scraps I can't use even for crumb quilts. When it gets full, I stitch it together and donate it to the animal shelter to use as pet pillows," Eva said.

"Oh, that's genius!" Sarah said. "I love that idea!"

"Me, too! I have some pillowcases I've been on the fence about keeping, and now I know exactly what to do with them," Jennifer said.

"It can take a while to fill them up, but it's always such a sense of accomplishment when I do, and the shelter appreciates the donation."

The ladies stopped to do a show and tell of their work before packing up their sewing machines and supplies. Eva had cut one of the ten-inch squares she'd made during the week into strips and was adding a narrow strip of black fabric in between, which set off the bright colors even more. Jennifer had embellished her piece with scraps of lace, ribbon, and rick rack for her crazy quilt. Annalise had sewn like colors together and was reassembling them into shapes to form an abstract landscape. Sarah had cut circles from her crumb piece and was appliqueing them onto a base of a solid color to make a mug rug, an oversize coaster big enough for a glass or cup and a snack to place beside it as well.

"Your piece has given me an idea for my journal cover," Eva told Jennifer. "Not exactly a crazy quilt, but I can add embellishments to the top of what I have to add some texture."

"This has been so much fun!" Annalise said. "I haven't felt this creative with my quilting in a while. Being together with all of you and sharing your energy is giving me even more inspiration."

"That's exactly how I feel!" Sarah agreed. "I can't wait to come back next week. I've been looking forward to this all day, and it has really helped me decompress after such a busy work week. I think Ashley was almost as excited as I was to have me leave the house for a while. I might have been a little bit cranky this week."

The others chuckled at her confession.

"I'm so glad I decided to come. I needed this break from all the sadness of the past week," Jennifer said.

"The encouragement and support we get from others is one of the things I love about having a hobby and sharing it with a group," Eva said.

"This group is going to be something special. I have a feeling," Annalise said and winked as everyone smiled.

After everyone had left, Reuben came into the living room to join Eva.

Is this going to be happening every week now?

"Yes, Reuben. Are you put out by the disruption to your routine?"

It's not like I have any say in it, now is there?

"Good point, so you might as well join the party.

Harrumph was all he said as he turned and stalked back out of the room, his displeasure evident. Eva chuckled, knowing he would come around eventually.

CHAPTER SEVEN

*T*he first rays of sunshine were only barely appearing in the sky when Eva awoke the next day, but the excitement of returning to the quilting project had taken hold. Knowing going back to sleep would not be an option, she began her day and was already several hours into her quilting project when Jim called.

"How was your quilting club meeting?"

"It was great! I'm finding a new passion for living again."

"Sounds like this was a good move for you."

"Absolutely! It's partly the creative process of quilting but being with this group of women has been a big part of it, too. We were surprised Jennifer showed up for last night's meeting, but she shared some news I wanted to run by you. She says the police are focusing on her cousin, Thomas, but she thinks they're barking up the wrong tree."

"I guess I'm not giving out any confidential information from what my poker buddies have told me if you already know that. Did she mention he doesn't have an alibi, and it looks like he and his grandmother may have had a disagreement the night she died?"

"She did, but she insists Thomas isn't doing drugs now and he loved his grandmother, so the idea he would have killed her for drug money isn't adding up. He's told them he only needed the money just temporarily so he could cover his rent."

"He does have a history of substance abuse making him a prime suspect for now."

"Did they find any other clues at the crime scene that might lead to someone else having been with Sadie?"

"Well, there was one possibility, but it might also tie her cousin into the crime scene even more instead of ruling him out."

"What was that?"

"They found a couple drops of blood which weren't Sadie's. They're not sure how it happened as there were no defensive wounds on Sadie's body to indicate she put up a fight, but the killer will have a wound of some type and the blood will provide DNA evidence. It will take a while to process, but even a blood type match would either tie him in or eliminate Thomas as being at the scene."

"Will they be asking him to give them a sample or provide proof of his blood type?"

"If he won't give it voluntarily, they'll have to get a court order."

"Did they say when that would be happening? I assume this isn't something I should mention to Jennifer. I wouldn't want it to come back on you for sharing the information with me."

"Yes, it was for your ears only. My guess is they'll be getting right on it. Today, if possible. That way, they can move on knowing they've got the wrong suspect if the blood type doesn't match."

"I won't say anything. Please let me know if you hear about any updates, though. It would be a huge relief for the family to not have that over their heads. Well, I guess unless the blood type matches, and you have to wait for a more conclusive DNA test."

"Yes, that's the rub. If his blood type is the same, he'll still be on the persons of interest list."

They finished up their conversation and Eva hung up; her mood no better than before she'd spoken with Jim.

You look like you lost your best friend.

"I'm worried about Jennifer's cousin, Thomas. He might be framed for a murder he didn't commit if no other evidence turns up to clear him."

Didn't the psychic convince you it's not him?

"I do want to believe her, but a psychic's feelings don't count for much in a court of law. They'll need something more scientifically based."

Maybe another witness will turn up.

"What makes you say that?"

Just a feeling.

Eva gave him a look.

What? You think only psychics can have a feeling?

Eva shook her head and walked back to her sewing studio.

CHAPTER EIGHT

*W*hen the growling of her stomach broke through the noise of her sewing machine, Eva checked the time and was surprised to find it was noon. She made herself a cup of coffee and an egg salad sandwich with a side of chips and a dill pickle. The TV had been set up to record the noon news, so she backed up the DVR to catch the ten minutes she'd missed while she was making her lunch.

In a bizarre twist to the Sadie Emerson murder of last week, her neighbor's body was discovered this morning by a Twin City Energy employee. The Penobscot County Sheriff's office confirmed the badly decomposed body of Howard Smith was found on his front porch when the delivery driver opened the door to leave the receipt for the propane delivery. An autopsy will be performed, but initial findings based on the state of decomposition indicate it is likely the death occurred the same night as that of Sadie Emerson. No suspects have been arrested for her murder and the investigation is ongoing.

The cause of a fatal motorcycle accident on Route 15 early this morning is being reported as likely due to excessive speed and alcohol consumption....

Eva turned off the TV and sat thinking about the news of Sadie's neighbor, her lunch only half-eaten. Two murders in her little town were news enough, but for both of them to have occurred on the same night to neighbors had to be connected somehow. But what was the connection? She hadn't known either Sadie or Howard Smith, but Jennifer was likely to have known Howard. She would have to call her later to inquire further since she would be at work now and this wasn't something appropriate to discuss during her office hours. She decided to call Annalise instead.

Annalise answered on the first ring.

"I just heard it on the news!" Annalise said as soon as she answered the phone.

Eva was taken aback but refrained from making any remarks about being psychic.

"Are you thinking this has to be related to Sadie's murder, too?"

"I don't see how it couldn't be," Annalise said. "The question is, who was killed first and was that why the second one was murdered? Were they an eyewitness who had to be gotten rid of?"

"That's what made the most sense to me, but then I remembered the time of night when they happened. Wouldn't it have been too dark to see anything?"

"Maybe not if they had one of those newer LED floodlights. Some of those can be as much as a million lumens."

"I have no idea how to put that into perspective, but it sounds powerful, and increases the chances someone could have witnessed what happened even at that time of night. I'm not sure how this fits into Jennifer's cousin's claim he couldn't have been involved, but the idea a serial killer might be out there isn't something I want to consider either."

Annalise didn't respond immediately, and Eva was about to check her phone to see if she'd lost the connection. She was about to ask Annalise if she was still on the line, when Annalise spoke.

"I don't have the sense that's what's going on here. The impression I'm getting is this wasn't premeditated. It was a random act, and the second murder was to cover the killer's tracks and silence the only witness."

"Do you know who was killed first?"

"No, it's not coming through clearly. Things don't always come to me in chronological sequence, so I can't say with certainty. And wouldn't want to say as it could influence any evidence we turn up later."

"We?" Eva asked, the surprise in her voice coming through loud and clear.

Annalise chuckled. "Why are you sounding so surprised? You're already involved, whether you realized it or not."

"How…. Oh, I guess I am, just not as actively as I was thinking about. Do you think there's more we can do?"

"I do. We all have gifts we can use that the police will never have. Do you think Sarah would agree to going to Sadie's house? She might be able to connect with Sadie."

Eva contemplated the question. She didn't know Sarah well, but under the circumstances, she thought she might be willing to help, especially since this was Jennifer's aunt.

"We can ask, but shouldn't we ask Jennifer how she feels about it first? She might not be agreeable and now that I think of it, she might need to ask her cousin's permission to go into Sadie's house. Explaining she wants to have a friend talk to her mother's ghost might not go over well. Not everyone is open to the possibility talking to spirits isn't a bunch of hooey."

"That's true. We could always wait until her cousin has gone back home. If the police haven't arrested a suspect by then, that is."

"I think that's the best idea," Eva said. "Have you ever been in a séance? I can't say I have."

"Yes, I have. I don't remember Sarah saying how she communicates with spirits, though. Let's ask her at the next Club meeting."

"Sounds like a plan. Now we've got that settled, how's your quilt coming?" Eva asked.

"I'm so excited about it! It's coming together great."

The ladies chatted for a few minutes more about their projects before wrapping up their conversation.

* * *

EVA SAT PONDERING the suggestion of asking Sarah to contact Sadie. The more she thought about it, the more she realized it would be better to ask Sarah before approaching Jennifer. She didn't want to dash Jennifer's hopes if this was something Sarah would be uncomfortable doing. Her mind made up, she found Sarah's name in her Contacts list and hit the Call button.

"This is Sarah Pascal."

"Hello, Sarah. This is Eva Perkins. Have I caught you at a bad time?"

"I have a Zoom meeting in half an hour, but I can talk now. What can I do for you?"

"Annalise and I had an idea. We were going to wait until the next meeting to bring it up to you and Jennifer, but after thinking about it, I realized it would be better to approach you first."

"What's the idea?"

"I hope this isn't out of line to ask, but we wondered if you might be willing to contact Sadie in case she might be able to identify her killer." Eva held her breath, unsure of what Sarah's response might be.

There was silence on the line, and Eva was afraid she might have crossed a line.

"It's not normally something I would agree to do, but for Jennifer, I'd be willing to try. Is she okay with this?"

Eva let out her breath in relief. At least the first hurdle had been crossed.

"As I mentioned, we were going to wait until the next meeting to bring it up with both of you. The more I thought about it, though, I realized if you were uncomfortable doing this, it wouldn't be fair to either you or Jennifer to put you in that position or get Jennifer's hopes up. And, of course, we want Jennifer to be comfortable with this, too."

"If Jennifer's okay with it, then so am I."

"Oh, that's wonderful, Sarah. Thank you so much!"

"Don't thank me yet," Sarah cautioned. "I might not be able to contact Sadie, even if Jennifer is willing to let me try."

"We'll cross that bridge when we come to it. At least we have something we can propose to Jennifer and let her take it from there."

"Sounds good. I'll see you on Tuesday."

Eva immediately called Annalise.

"Sarah agreed to try to contact Sadie," she announced after they'd exchanged their greetings. "It occurred to me if she wasn't, it might disappoint Jennifer or put Sarah on the spot if we sprung it on her at the meeting."

"Good thinking. It does make more sense her to be on board first, now that you say it."

"Cross your fingers Jennifer is willing to give it a try and Sadie can tell Sarah who it was."

"Fingers crossed."

CHAPTER NINE

"*If* you would grill the burgers, I'll finish up the salad and set the table," Eva told Jim at dinnertime that evening.

"Happy to do it," Jim said, taking the plate of burgers, cheese slices, and buns from Eva and headed to the back deck where the grill was located.

The aroma of grilling burgers wafted in through the screen door where Reuben sat watching.

I don't suppose you're going to share any of those, are you?

"You know I'm not. Dr. Adams gave me strict orders to watch your diet and no treats!"

Reuben narrowed his eyes before turning his head back to resume watching Jim's efforts, and his tail twitched as though to emphasize his displeasure at the response, but he didn't argue further.

Ten minutes later, Jim came back into the house with the cheeseburgers, and they sat down to eat their meal.

"Do you have any news you can share about the Howard Smith murder?" Eva asked.

"Well, it's only a preliminary finding until they complete the autopsy, but it looks like it was murder, and the cause of death was blunt force trauma to the head, just like with Sadie Emerson. The murder weapon wasn't found at that crime scene either, so it's still not conclusive whether Howard or Sadie was the first victim or how their murders are connected."

"Do they think it's a case of a potential witness being murdered to cover the killer's tracks?"

"That's one theory, for sure. Howard Smith wasn't a very likeable person, but he didn't have any obvious enemies the police are aware of. He was one of those irascible, cranky types who kept to himself and preferred everyone keep their distance, too, so he could do what he wanted without interference. Neighbors have complained to the Town Office about his having unlicensed vehicles in his back yard because he'd exceeded the two allowed by the town. They found a citation from the Code Enforcement Officer in Howard's hand, so the police are questioning him in case he might have seen something when he was there or have information which would help them."

"You don't think the Code Enforcement Officer would have done it, do you?"

"No. Stephen Hill doesn't strike me as the murderer type. He's not being considered as a person of interest."

"It seems like he would have come forward before this if he knew anything about either of the murders. Now that I think about it, wouldn't they already have questioned him about whether he saw or heard anything? If I remember correctly, he lives on the other side of Sadie, so he's also a neighbor to both Sadie and Howard," Eva said.

"I'd forgotten that, but yes. Sadie lived between Howard and Stephen. If Howard was already dead, he would have called the police. Nine o'clock isn't terribly late, but it doesn't seem like he'd be out that late at night to be handing out citations, either."

They both fell quiet as they finished their meal, each

wrapped in their own thoughts about who might have been the murderer.

"Have the police let the family go back into Sadie's house?" Eva asked after a few minutes.

"Yes, the CSI units have finished up their investigation. Why do you ask?"

"No reason in particular. Jennifer mentioned her house felt a little crowded with her cousin still here. If the house was available, they could stay there now instead."

"That makes sense. They might not want to, though. Some people aren't comfortable being in a house where someone has died, and it's even worse if they were murdered, especially when they were related to the victim."

"I guess I can understand. From what I've heard, though, Sadie was a gentle woman who wouldn't hurt a flea. I can't imagine being a ghost would change that," she said.

"Don't tell me you believe in ghosts."

"I believe in the *possibility* of ghosts," Eva responded with a wink.

"I can't argue with that."

CHAPTER TEN

$\mathcal{E}$va arrived at Sarah's house on Saturday, as planned. It was a two-story older home in the "trees" section of Bangor, which got its nickname because the streets were named for various types of trees. The house itself was well-maintained, but Eva had to agree with Sarah the landscaping needed an update.

Sarah greeted Eva with a hug as she opened the door and invited her inside.

"Thank you so much for coming. Ashley and I really appreciate your offer to help. She's in the kitchen."

Eva followed Sarah past the stairway directly to the left of the doorway. On the right was a living room which opened to the dining room and the kitchen was straight ahead down a short hallway. It had been updated recently and had a warm, cozy ambiance. Ashley was sitting at a table placed in the center of the room rather than an island, as was the current style trend for kitchens. Sitting next to her was a Golden Retriever who sat up as soon as he spied Eva and gave her a short bark of greeting.

"Well, hello to you, too. What's your name?" Eva asked him.

He gave another bark, and Sarah looked at Eva with the

unspoken question of whether she should tell Ashley what was going on between them.

"Sure, that's okay," Eva replied, before turning her attention back to the dog. "I'm happy to meet you, Max. My name is Eva." She held out her hand palm down for Max to sniff, which he did before giving it a lick as well.

Ashley turned a bewildered look at Sarah.

"Eva can communicate with animals," she explained.

"Ohhh," Ashley turned back to Eva, but the announcement did not seem to faze her, which Eva assumed had a lot to do with knowing about Sarah's ability to communicate with ghosts. She held out her hand to Eva. "I'm Ashley, but I'm guessing you already know that."

"I assumed as much, but nice to meet you, Ashley," she smiled, shaking Ashley's hand. "You have a lovely home. How long have you lived here?"

"We bought the house three years ago. We've spent most of our time renovating the inside and finally have it done so are ready to tackle the outside."

"Would you like to take a look at the back yard? That's where we need the most help, although the front is in need of some curb appeal, too."

"Sure, lead the way."

Sarah led the way out the door which opened to the back yard from the kitchen. It was a typical small city lot and other than a patch of sad looking grass with more brown spots than green, there was no other vegetation. The yard had been fenced with a cedar stockade style fence that appeared to be recently installed to provide privacy and a safe space for Max.

"I guess this is what you call a blank slate," Eva joked.

"You are being kind," Sarah replied.

"My first question is how you would like to use the space, followed by how much time do you want to put into upkeep?"

"Follow up question should probably be can you keep plants alive?" Ashley addedBetty.

"Good information to have," Eva agreed.

"Honestly, we're both novices, so having low maintenance plants might be the best way to start out until we improve our gardening skills. We would definitely like to have an area for seating and to put the BBQ grill. Some flowers would be nice, but easy upkeep and any that can be planted once and come back every year would be great. We both have jobs that keep us busy, and Ashley's job requires traveling, so we don't have a lot of extra time. "

"It's a little late to put in a vegetable garden this year, but is it something you'd like to do in the future?"

Sarah and Ashley exchanged glances, and both shook their heads.

"We might change our minds later, but we could always add it then, couldn't we?"

"Absolutely! A small, raised bed can be added anytime. I have a few ideas but would like to give it some more thought. How about if I sketch out a plan and give it to you at the next Club meeting?"

"That would be wonderful. In the meantime, let's go back inside. Ashley made brownies for us, if you're interested."

"You don't have to twist my arm."

"Come on, Max. Time to go in," Sarah called, and Max turned from his inspection of the far corner of the lot to bound after them.

"What do you do for work, Ashley? Sarah mentioned you have to travel," Eva asked after they'd settled at the table with drinks and the plate of brownies.

"I'm a licensed pharmacist, but my current position is as a district manager for one of the national drugstore chains. It sometimes requires me to visit the actual stores to assist the store managers for my territory, which includes all the stores from Augusta to the northern border of the state."

"That's a lot of area to cover."

"It is. It's not so much the number of stores involved as it is the distance to drive to some of them. Fortunately, it isn't an everyday thing, but there are times I have to be away for a day or two at a time."

"Were you aware of Sarah's ability to communicate with ghosts before you got married?"

"No, we'd been married a year and had known each other for four years before that. It wasn't until we attended her grandmother's funeral. I knew Sarah was upset but figured it was an obvious reaction, so when I saw her in almost a trance state at one point during the service and she wasn't responding to my attempts to ask her if she was okay, it freaked me out. I finally waited until she seemed to come back to herself. Once we were back outside the church and away from the others so we wouldn't be overheard, I asked her about it. At first, she was reluctant to tell me what had happened, but I can be persuasive," she said, looking at Sarah with affection.

"I'd had pretty much the same experience as you growing up, Eva. Kids made fun of me when they would see me talking to no one and called me a weirdo when I tried to give them messages from relatives who had passed on. Adults would react even worse, especially if I passed along information or a message that struck a chord. It didn't take long for me to keep it to myself, which can be difficult and scary when you're a kid and you have a persistent ghost wanting to get their words heard by the living."

"I can only imagine. Conversations with animals seem almost normal compared to that."

"For a while, it stopped. I guess they realized there wasn't any point trying if I wasn't going to pass on their messages. It wasn't until my grandmother passed when it started again. Having Ashley to confide in helped me to be receptive again, and I've learned some ways of passing along a message so I don't have to explain how I got it."

"I hope you're able to connect with Sadie. That is, if Jennifer agrees to our suggestion to have you try."

"Me, too. I want to do everything I can to help her."

"Something just occurred to me. Do you think Howard Smith might try to contact you, too?" Eva asked. "They were neighbors, after all. Maybe he would want to tell someone about what happened to him. Or is that even how this works?"

"I suppose it's possible. Getting justice for his death is information I would think he'd want someone to know."

"I'm thinking the same thing," Eva agreed. "Well, I should head back home. Thank you for the delicious brownie and the visit. It was good to get to know you a little better outside of the quilt club. And to meet you, Ashley. And, of course, you, Max," Eva added when Max gave a short bark as he looked up at her from beside her chair. "I'll give you my ideas about plants that should work for you when I see you on Tuesday."

"I'm looking forward to it."

CHAPTER ELEVEN

"*D*o you already have something planned for dinner?" Jim asked after he and Eva had said their helloes.

"I had some leftovers but what do you have in mind?"

"I don't feel like cooking and I thought you might like to join me at The Checkout Diner."

The Checkout Diner was Glen Lake's sole eating establishment. The décor was typical diner style, but the food was decent and the prices reasonable. It was also in the same building as the town's only convenience store, separated by a partial wall with a large, cased door entry enabling customers to go back and forth between them.

"I like your thinking. When should I be ready for you to pick me up?"

"Is fifteen minutes too soon?"

"Not at all. I'll see you then."

Eva was waiting outside when Jim pulled into her driveway. She waved Jim off as he started to get out of the car, knowing he was going to open the car door for her. She didn't have a problem with him doing it, but there were times when that level of courtesy felt excessive.

"How was your day?" Jim asked when Eva had gotten in and buckled her seatbelt.

"It was fun. I went to my Club member Sarah's house in Bangor. She had asked me to give her some ideas for landscaping after she had seen my gardens. I got to meet her wife, Ashley, and their dog, Max."

"Were you able to give her any tips?"

"Some, but I'm going to think about it and give her more suggestions at our next meeting. How was your day?"

"Quiet. I mowed the lawn which was the highlight of my day… until now," he said looking over at her with a grin.

"Oh, please," she teased, giving him an eyeroll.

Eva's house was only three miles away, so it didn't take long for them to reach the diner. The parking lot only had one car on the diner side of the building.

"Looks like we got here at a good time," Jim said, and this time Eva waited for him to open the car door for her.

The interior of the diner had a long counter with seating, three booths on the left side of the entrance, and to the right were six tables with four chairs at each.

"Go ahead and seat yourselves," the diner's waitress, Betty Jones, called out from behind the counter. Betty was a fifty-ish aged woman, a bit on the short side at five feet, four inches, with dyed blonde hair and blue eyes. She'd worked at the diner for at least fifteen years and had a reputation for being the town crier. If anyone would know something about the local chatter, it would be her.

It wasn't necessary for them to discuss where they should sit. At this point in their relationship, they knew they both preferred a booth if one was available. Eva led the way to the one farthest from the door and Jim took the side opposite her facing the front of the diner.

"How are you two doing today?" Betty asked, handing them a menu after putting a glass of water on the table for each of them.

"Can't complain but if I did, no one would listen anyway," Jim winked at her.

"Never heard that one before," she said, her voice dripping with sarcasm.

Eva chuckled and so did Jim.

"The specials are up on the board. I'll give you a few minutes to decide."

"Do you think she might have heard any gossip about who killed Sadie?" Eva asked Jim.

"I'm sure she has, but that's probably all it is. Gossip."

Eva didn't push the topic with Jim but made up her mind to ask Betty anyway when she came back to take their orders.

"What's the word around town about who might have killed Sadie Emerson?" she asked as soon as Betty returned to their booth.

"Only one name has come up that might actually be worth looking into, but I don't know if anyone has mentioned him to the police. Howard Smith and Greg Ellingwood have had a feud for years. Greg lives on the other side of Howard."

Jim and Eva nodded to acknowledge they knew who he was and where he lived when Betty paused.

"Greg has been upset about all the junk cars Howard had in his yard. He claimed he was going to fix them up to sell them, but he never did. It made Greg madder than a hornet. He thought it was devaluing his property to have what he called a junkyard right next to his. He would file a complaint with the town if it went on too long. The code enforcement officer... that's been Stephen Hill for, oh, close to ten years now... would talk to Howard to remind him he was only allowed to have two at a time and he was violating the town ordinance by having too many unlicensed vehicles. Howard would usually get rid of some of them, and things would calm down for awhile. Lately, though, he'd been ignoring Stephen's warnings and Greg said he had had enough. He was going to take matters into his own hands even if it meant dealing with Howard himself if the town wasn't going to do anything about it."

"Do you think Greg would have taken it that far?" Eva asked.

"Well, both Howard and Greg had a reputation for their bad tempers. I *might* be able to see him getting into it with Howard and things getting out of hand. I don't know how that would fit with Sadie's murder, though. She didn't have anything to do with their arguments. Do you think there could be two murderers?"

"It's possible," Jim said, "but I'm not sure if that's the case here. The police seem to think they're related."

"Oh," Betty said, and her shoulders slumped. "Maybe they don't know about the feud between Howard and Greg, though, so they're not looking at it from that angle," she said, her face brightening with that possibility, reluctant to give up after having her theory shot down.

"Have you mentioned it to them?" Jim asked.

"Well, no," Betty said, flustered.

"It might not turn out to be anything, but it wouldn't hurt to tell them in case they're not aware of it. If nothing else, they would want to speak to Greg since he was Howard's neighbor, if they haven't already."

Betty considered his suggestion and then bobbed her head once she had made her decision. "I'm going to do that the next time Deputy Tremblay comes in!" she said, standing a little taller and with a determined expression. "Now, what can I get you folks to eat?"

CHAPTER TWELVE

"I thought we could start this week by doing a show and tell of how our projects are coming along," Eva announced when everyone had finished their potluck dinner and the next meeting of the Cozy Quilts Club began. "I have mine almost finished, except for the hand stitching."

"Your journal cover turned out great, Eva," Jennifer said as Annalise and Sarah nodded their heads in agreement. "I've been having fun with my project. The combination of a crumb quilt with a crazy quilt has been a great way to use up not only my fabric scraps but lace and ribbons as well. I haven't decided yet if I'll put it in a frame or add a hanging sleeve. What do you all think?"

"Have you considered using a shadow box frame?" Sarah asked.

"Ooh, I like that idea," Annalise agreed.

"Me, too," Eva concurred.

"Problem solved," Jennifer replied with a smile.

Annalise was next. "I decided to do a lake landscape. It's not as scrappy as most crumb quilting, but I still used different scraps to put together the colors I needed, and I was able to create depth with the gradients of color. It worked especially well for the blues for the lake."

"Did you use an iron on interfacing to attach the pieces to a backing like an applique?" Jennifer asked.

"Yes, that's exactly the process. I left them raw edged and when I do the quilting, I'll go over those to make sure they're attached well. I'd planned to put a hanging sleeve on the back but may go with putting it in a frame instead.

"My project looks uninspired after seeing all of yours, but I didn't want to make anything too complicated while my day job is taking so much time this month. I've only done a few random circles for my mug rug, and it's still needing hand stitching at the opening to turn it out and then edgestitch around," Sarah said.

"Or you can edgestitch the opening closed at the same time and save yourself a step," Eva suggested.

"Duh, of course! I'm so glad I didn't put the extra work into that. I had avoided using a binding to finish it off to save myself some time. Why I didn't realize I could just stitch around to finish it…"

"That's why you have us," Jennifer said.

"Have you spoken to any of your neighbors about Sadie's and Howard Smith's murders?" Eva asked Jennifer.

"I had a chance to talk to Stephen Hill last night when I was checking up on Sadie's house. My cousin needed to go back to Massachusetts to check on her own house, but will be back again in a couple of weeks. It has us both nervous about a possible serial killer still on the loose. Stephen told me he'd had to go to the convenience store that night and since he was out anyway, stopped on his way home to give Howard the citation for having too many unregistered vehicles in his yard. No one had answered the doorbell or responded to his knocks, so he'd left the citation tucked in the inside door on the porch and went back to his own house. Stephen didn't know if Howard was actually at home and ignoring him or if he came back after Stephen left to go back to his house. He didn't remember if Sadie's lights were on or not, but since Howard's body was on the porch when the propane delivery driver found him, and when the police think he and Sadie were killed, it had to be shortly afterwards."

Eva glanced over at Annalise, who nodded encouragingly for her to speak up.

"Annalise and I were wondering what you would think about Sarah going to Sadie's house. I've asked Sarah, and she's okay with it if you are," she said, looking at Sarah. "Maybe she could make contact with Sadie to get a description of her killer."

"Oh, it hadn't even occurred to me, but if you're willing to do that, Sarah, I think it would be worth a try. The police haven't come up with any new leads, even after finding Howard's body."

"Have they decided your cousin isn't a suspect anymore?" Annalise asked.

"Yes, he'd forgotten he had ordered a pizza that arrived at the time Sadie was murdered and once they verified his story, it gave him the alibi he needed. The delivery driver recognized his photo as the person who answered the door. He'd been so nervous when the police first questioned him because of his past arrest, he didn't think of it until afterwards. I didn't think he was guilty, but it's an enormous relief for all of us he's no longer a suspect. He loved Sadie and his drug days are behind him, but without the alibi, they could have made the case he'd argued over money, especially with the incriminating texts sent between him and Sadie."

"I can't promise to get results, Jennifer, but if you're okay with it, I'm happy to help."

"I'm on the fence," Jennifer answered. "Finding Sadie's murderer is a top priority, but I'm not sure about contacting her about it. I've never done anything like this before. I guess if she doesn't want to be contacted, she wouldn't appear to you, right?" she asked Sarah.

"That's been my experience. Spirits communicate with me

because they want to be heard. We can go into Sadie's house and if she allows her presence to be known, then fine, but I won't force it."

"That's fair. I'm okay with doing it on those conditions."

"Can you meet me at her house after work tomorrow, say around five-thirty?"

Sarah checked her phone's calendar to make sure she didn't have a meeting before agreeing.

"Would it be okay if Annalise and I come, too? Or would that be too much? I'd love to see how this works in real life."

"Me too," Annalise joined in.

"I've never had an audience, but I guess it would be okay. If it feels like it isn't working because there's a crowd, I can always have you wait outside and see if that makes a difference."

The ladies' excitement grew about the possibility of having Sadie communicate with Sarah and possibly solving the murder, but they managed to work on their projects for the rest of the club meeting.

CHAPTER THIRTEEN

*T*he group met at Sadie's house the next day at five-thirty, as planned. They filed into the house after Jennifer unlocked the door and stood in a huddle, not knowing what the next move should be.

"Where did you find Sadie?" Sarah asked, breaking the silence.

"She was about where you are now. Boscoe was right beside her as though he was making sure she wouldn't be alone," Jennifer said, her voice catching with emotion.

"Maybe if the rest of you sit down over there and I'll stay here to see if Sadie wants to make contact," Sarah suggested.

They all found seats on the couch and chairs nearby, waiting and trying not to add any pressure to Sarah to make a connection with Sadie. A few minutes passed and Eva was beginning to wonder if there were too many people in the room, or maybe Sadie had passed on to her next realm and didn't want to communicate.

"My name is Sarah."

The other ladies sat up, looking at each other as though to question whether any of them saw an ethereal presence in the room. They all shook their heads to answer the unspoken question.

"I'm a friend of Jennifer's. I'm here to ask if you can help us identify your killer. The police don't have any leads." Sarah was focusing on a spot a couple feet in front of her, clearly seeing someone not visible to the others. Only she could hear Sadie speaking as the words were forming inside her head rather than aloud.

I'd let Boscoe out to do his business and he was barking at something I couldn't see. It looked like he was focused on Howard Smith's house. Howard's porch light was on and there might have been someone else with him, but I couldn't see clearly. My night vision isn't good anymore. I called Boscoe in and locked the back door and was getting ready to go to bed when someone knocked on my front door. At first, I wasn't going to answer, but he knocked again and when I peeked out the window, I saw...

CHAPTER FOURTEEN

*E*veryone jumped when there was a knock on the door. Jennifer hurried over to answer and opened the door to find Stephen Hill there.

"Is everything okay? I saw the cars in the driveway but didn't recognize them and wanted to make sure no one was in here who shouldn't be," he said, his view of the others blocked by the partially open door.

"Everything's fine," Jennifer told him, moving to block his view as he attempted to look around her. "Thanks for checking, though, Stephen. It's so nice of you to be looking out for Sadie even now."

"Well, okay, I'll be on my way," Stephen said when he realized Jennifer wasn't going to invite him in or offer any additional information.

Jennifer stood at the window, watching until Stephen walked back toward his house.

"That was odd. I don't remember him ever checking up on Sadie's house before."

"Did you notice the bandage on his arm?" Eva asked.

"I did," Annalise replied. "I thought something was off about it but why do you ask?"

"Just a feeling I had, too. I remembered Jim told me the CSI team had found a couple drops of blood on the floor that weren't Sadie's at the crime scene." She realized as soon as the words were out of her mouth, it was a mistake. "I wasn't supposed to know that. Please don't repeat it to anyone else or it would get Jim in a lot of trouble."

"I won't," they all said, almost in unison.

"Do you think Stephen might be a suspect?" Jennifer asked Sarah, her eyes wide.

"I lost my connection with Sadie when he knocked. She was about to tell me who had come to her door. I'm not sensing her presence here now, so I don't think I'll be able to find out anything more today. I think Howard Smith might have been about to join us, along with Sadie. I could feel another presence in the background, but it went away at the same time as Sadie."

The disappointment registered on all their faces.

"What did she say to you?" Jennifer asked.

"She told me Boscoe had been barking at something he was seeing at Howard Smith's house. She thought she might have seen someone else with him on his porch, but it was too dark to tell for sure. She had been locking up for the night when she heard the knock on her front door, and she opened it because she recognized the person who was standing outside. That's all I got because we were interrupted. We were so close, though. She was just about to tell me who it was."

"I guess we might as well lock up, then. Do you think we could try again later?" Jennifer asked Sarah.

"It wasn't a strong connection, but I'd be willing to try."

Discouraged but not defeated, the group left.

CHAPTER FIFTEEN

"*We* haven't gone on a day trip in weeks. Is this a good time for you to get away?" Jim asked.

"Let me check my calendar. You're in luck. It looks like my schedule is flexible today. What do you have in mind?"

"How about Camden? It's a beautiful day to be by the ocean and we could grab some lunch. Maybe do some looking around in those shops you like."

Eva knew the offer was a sacrifice on Jim's part. To say he wasn't a shopper would be an understatement. Neither was Eva, for that matter, but would make an exception when she had the opportunity to check out independent shops featuring hand-crafted and locally sourced items.

"Sounds great! Should I drive to your house, or will you come here to pick me up?"

"I'll pick you up. Can you be ready in twenty minutes?"

"Not a problem. All I need to do is grab my purse and lock up, so I'll be ready whenever you get here."

"See you soon."

"Looks like you'll have the house to yourself today, Reuben," Eva said after disconnecting the call.

That suits me just fine. You have had way too many people in here disrupting my routine lately.

"Poor baby."

Your sympathy is overwhelming he said before turning his back on her to look out the window.

Realizing that was her cue to be dismissed, Eva went to the bathroom to check her hair and put on mascara and lipstick before Jim arrived.

She heard the knock on the door before Jim let himself in and noted Reuben hadn't alerted her he arrived. *"He really must have his nose out of joint,"* she thought.

She hurried out of the bathroom and picked up her purse from its hook on her closet door, and went out to greet Jim.

"Sorry, I know I said I'd be ready before you got here, but I wanted to spruce up a little more for you," she said, giving him a grin.

"You didn't have to do that for me. You always look pretty."

Oh, brother. Could you lay it on any thicker? Reuben said, sitting upright in his spot in the window seat.

If cats were able to roll their eyes, Eva imagined Reuben would be doing that now. She kept her attention on Jim instead, not giving Reuben the satisfaction of acknowledging his remark.

"Thank you! I knew there was a reason I kept you around," Eva teased.

"Hopefully, it's not the only reason."

"Definitely not," Eva said, giving him a kiss on the cheek. "Let's take this show on the road." She nudged Jim toward the door and only as she turned to pull it closed did she look in Reuben's direction. By then, he had taken up his seat on his cushion in the window and ignored her in typical cat fashion.

Bye, Reuben. I'll see you in a few hours.

He turned, giving her a blink of his eyes. *Take your time. I'm going to enjoy the peace and quiet.*

Jim was giving her an appraising look. "Did you forget something?"

"No, why do you ask?"

"You took a long time closing the door. It seemed like you were looking at something and thinking hard about what it might be."

"Huh. I didn't realize I was doing that," she brushed off the question and headed for the passenger side of Jim's car.

Shrugging, he followed behind her, realizing there was no point questioning her further, but he filed it away at the back of his mind. *Time to take it out of cop mode, Jim. Sometimes a cigar is just a cigar.*

It was a beautiful early summer day with a nearly cloudless bright blue sky. One of many benefits of being retired was the ability to take day trips during the week and avoiding the weekend crowds. They encountered only light traffic which didn't slow them down as they made their way through the small, quintessentially New England towns. Many of them still had houses built close to two hundred years ago. Some would have been regal mansions in their heyday, built in a somewhat Italianate style and complete with widow's walks. They had been owned by lumber barons and shipping magnates who became rich from the lumber and shipbuilding industries of the 1800s. They were now showing their age and neglect, as the cost of repairs and maintenance outstripped the financial circumstances of their current owners.

"It makes me sad to see those old houses so shabby," Eva said after they passed by one of them which had caught her attention.

"They must have been showstoppers in their day," Jim agreed.

"Have you heard any updates on Sadie's and Howard's murders?" Eva asked after a pause in their conversation.

"Not really. Once they eliminated the grandson as a suspect, they ran out of leads. They're still on the case, but without any new information and no witnesses coming forward, there's only so much they can do."

"Did anything come of the blood spots that weren't Sadie's?" Eva asked.

"Not that I know of, but getting DNA results takes a while. With no suspect to match them to, they have no urgency to rush to get the testing done."

Realizing Jim had no other relevant information to pass along and seeing they were approaching Camden's downtown area, Eva let that line of questioning go.

"Looks like we're going to be lucky finding a parking spot within easy walking distance," Jim said as he slid the car into a spot. "Should we have lunch first and then do the walk and shop?"

"I could eat now. Plus, that way we can eat dessert and walk off the calories so we won't feel guilty."

"I like the way you think," Jim said, giving her a smile and taking her hand in his.

They walked a short distance to the center of downtown with the Penobscot Bay directly in front of them, the water a deep blue and calm with sunlight glinting off its surface. Shops, restaurants, and galleries catering primarily to the tourist trade lined both sides of the street. The architecture had remained true to its roots, giving it the feel of still being in the past and characteristically coastal New England style.

"Oh, look at how pretty it is in the harbor," Eva exclaimed, taking in the view of the Bay speckled with boats of all types, although today it was predominantly sailboats and even a yacht here and there. Camden had been a force in the schooner shipbuilding industry in the 1800s and had remained vibrant in large part because of its scenic beauty. Two of the windjammers built then were still in service, taking passengers on weeklong cruises. It had been a location site for nearly two dozen movies over the years and later in the summer, it would be thronged with out of state visitors. They had come at just the right time to avoid those crowds, making it much easier to find a table at one of the waterfront restaurants.

Once seated in the outside dining area at their favorite restaurant, The Waterfront, they sat enjoying the view of the harbor and soaking up the warmth of the sun, which felt especially nice after a long Maine winter.

"I could spend the rest of the day right here," Eva said with a sigh.

"Does that mean you want to skip the shopping?"

"Not on your life. I probably won't get another chance all summer to do this, so I better take advantage of the occasion. I promise I won't linger too long, though," she said, giving him some hope of a reprieve.

"That's okay. I'm the one who offered, so you take all the time you want," and meant it.

Their appetizer orders arrived then. They had decided to share an order of the local crab and artichoke fondue, followed up with the haddock tacos for Eva and grilled salmon burger for Jim.

"Do you suppose Betty ever mentioned the feud between Howard Smith and Greg Ellingwood to Deputy Tremblay?" Eva asked.

"I completely forgot to tell you about that. I heard through the grapevine she did, but Greg has a solid alibi so he's off the list of suspects."

"So Stephen Hill is a possibility," Eva thought. Aloud she said, "I thought it might be a longshot but it's too bad it didn't give them more to work with."

"I agree. They haven't given up, though."

"I know I mentioned walking off dessert, but I don't think I can eat another bite," Eva groaned when she was done.

"Me, either. How about if we walk around and find an ice cream shop if we're still craving something sweet later?"

"That sounds perfect."

"Where would you like to start?" Jim asked once they were back on the street.

"Why don't we take a left and walk up to the shop that's the farthest away and then work our way back down so we end up near where we parked?"

"That makes perfect sense," Jim said.

They spent the next three hours wandering from one boutique and gallery to the next until they were back to where they started.

"Are you ready for the ice cream yet?" Jim asked.

"I am! And then I think I'm ready to head back home. My feet are killing me."

"You won't get any argument from me."

"This was a great idea, Jim," Eva said, licking the side of her ice cream cone before it melted on her hand as she reached out with her other one to climb into the car.

"I agree. I enjoy spending time with you and wouldn't mind doing more of it."

Eva wasn't sure how to respond. When they'd first started dating, they had agreed they needed a lot of personal space and she had thought it was working for both of them. She wasn't sure she wanted to renegotiate the terms, at least not yet. *You're making more of this than there needs to be,* she scolded herself. *He wasn't asking to move in with you.* Jim didn't seem upset she hadn't replied, so she stayed quiet. The silence still felt companionable as they drove back home, and her anxiety was forgotten.

"Would you like to come in for coffee?" Eva offered when they parked in her driveway.

"Thanks, but I think I'll go home and stretch out. I'm not sure I'll be getting back up again once I put my feet up."

"I know what you mean."

She gave him a kiss and got out of the car, turning to give him a wave as he pulled out of the driveway. Reuben was trotting over to her as she opened the door.

About time you got home.

"What happened to the needing some peace and quiet you were complaining about when I left? Might be you like having me around more than you want to admit, Reuben."

No other answer was needed as he rubbed against her legs and began to purr.

CHAPTER SIXTEEN

$\mathcal{T}$he next day, Eva was back at her sewing machine, making more crumb quilt pieces to use up the rest of her small scraps. She wouldn't need them for this month's Club project, but she had been motivated to finish piecing all the remaining scraps into pieces she could use in a later project. It didn't require a lot of concentration, so her mind was able to wander. Thinking about the group's meeting at Sadie's house, something she couldn't quite put her finger on kept nagging at her in the back of her mind when suddenly it came to her. Boscoe had been there the whole time when the murder occurred. She might be able to get some answers to the mystery of who was with them by communicating with Boscoe. Perhaps if she and Sarah communicated separately with Sadie and Boscoe and the killer's name matched, then they would have corroboration. Excited by the idea, Eva couldn't wait to check with Jennifer to ask if Boscoe was home from the vet's and would she let her meet him. She texted in case Jennifer was at work and couldn't take a phone call.

> I had an idea that might be crazy, but is Boscoe home and doing better? He might be able to tell me more about who was there the night Sadie was murdered.

Jennifer must have had her phone handy, as Eva didn't have long to wait for a response.

> What a great idea! I can't believe none of us thought of it until now. He is back with us and seems to be better although not 100%. Would you like to come by tonight, say around 6:30?

> That should work. I'll see you then.

Eva arrived at Jennifer's house and was greeted by her at the door.

"Come on in. Boscoe is in the living room."

Jennifer led the way and they found Boscoe lying on his bed. He lifted his head to see who was there and rolled over onto his belly to look at Eva, assessing whether she was friend or foe, but didn't get up.

"Well, hello, Boscoe, my name is Eva," Eva said, bending down and holding her hand out palm down for Boscoe to sniff.

Hello, Eva. Are you a friend of Jennifer's?

"I am," she said to Boscoe. "He asked if I'm a friend of yours," she said to Jennifer.

Jennifer smiled and gave Boscoe a gentle pat on his head. "That's wild! Have you always been able to communicate with animals?"

"Ever since I was a little girl. It's easier for me with some than others, especially cats and dogs. I think that's because they're around humans so much."

"I hope you're able to have better luck than Sarah did."

"Me, too. We were so close. I have to caution you, though, that even if we do find out who the killer is, it's not like we can go to the police. As soon as I said Sadie's dog told me, they'd stop listening. We'll still have to find another way to reveal his identity."

"Ohh, of course. I got so excited about the idea of learning who it was I didn't think beyond that. It's still not a waste of time, though. If we know who killed her, we can find the way to force him to confess or lead the police to the clues so they would make an arrest."

"Fingers crossed," Eva said, holding up her crossed fingers.

"Boscoe, can you tell me what happened the night Sadie was killed?" Eva asked.

Sadie had let me out to do my business before we were going to sleep for the night. I saw the light on Howard Smith's porch and someone else was with him. They were arguing, but I don't think Sadie could hear them, and I don't think she saw them either. I tried barking, but she didn't understand. She called me back in, so I gave up. We were walking down the hall to her bedroom when there was a knock on the door. Sadie peeked out the window and then she opened the door to let whoever it was inside. The next thing I remember is waking up and Sadie was lying on the floor beside me. I tried waking her up, but it was no use, so I waited for someone to find us. It wasn't until the next day that Jennifer came.

"You don't remember who came in?"

"No. It's all fuzzy after the knock on the door and my head still hurts. I think Sadie knew who it was, but I can't remember what happened then."

Eva could tell he was becoming upset. She knew it was because he wanted to help and was frustrated by his loss of memory of what happened.

"It's alright, Boscoe. Maybe we can try again later when you're feeling better."

Boscoe didn't say any more but licked Eva's hand, letting her know he was grateful to finally be able to share what he did remember.

"I think we should let him rest for now. He told me the same story Sadie had told Sarah, but he can't remember what happened after Sadie opened the door. He said his head still hurts and his memory is fuzzy between Sadie opening the door and waking up beside her after they'd been attacked. Maybe after he's had more time to recuperate, the rest of what happened that night will come back to him and we can try again."

Jennifer's disappointment showed but she nodded her head in understanding.

"It was worth a shot," she said. "I can let you know when he's better if you think you'd like to try again."

"I still think it's a good idea. We just tried too soon."

CHAPTER SEVENTEEN

*T*wo days later Eva received a call from Jennifer to tell her Boscoe was doing much better.

"It's almost like a switch was flipped after you came to talk to him. He had mostly been sleeping on his bed after he got back from the vet's, but yesterday he was walking around and looked like he was back to his old self. I almost called you then, but I wanted to give it another day to make sure it wasn't a fluke. Do you think you could come over later this afternoon to speak with him again..." she hesitated and then continued. "Sorry, that sounds so weird to ask someone about having a conversation with a dog."

Eva chuckled.

"I have no doubt. Sure, I can come by. Maybe around four o'clock?"

"That would be perfect."

Eva parked her car in Jennifer's driveway at the appointed time and was about to walk to her door when it opened, and Jennifer came out with Boscoe on a leash.

"I saw you pull in. After we talked this morning, I had the idea it might help if we were at Sadie's house," Jennifer said.

"That's a great idea! If I think it's causing him too much distress, I'll stop immediately. We can always try again after he's had more time to heal."

After waiting for two cars to pass, they were able to cross the road and let themselves into Sadie's house.

Boscoe began sniffing the spot where Sadie had been found and whined, looking up at Jennifer.

"Are you alright to be here, Boscoe? We were hoping you might be able to remember what happened after Sadie opened the door if you were here at the house. If that's upsetting you, we can go back to Jennifer's."

"It's making me sad, but I remember the rest of it now. After you left before, I was thinking about that night and all of a sudden, it all came back to me."

"Can you tell me what happened?"

"Like I said, Sadie opened the door, and he came in and then he hit her on the head with a metal bar that was turned up on one end and had a notch on the other. I barked and bit him on his arm, but he hit me on the head, too. That's why I couldn't remember before. My head was hurting too much."

"I'm glad you're better now. Did you recognize the person who hit you and Sadie?"

Oh, of course.

CHAPTER EIGHTEEN

"*C*an you tell me their name?" Eva asked, trying not to sound impatient when Boscoe wasn't immediately forthcoming with that information.

It was our neighbor, Stephen Hill. Why would he do that? He and Sadie had always gotten along before, and he had no reason to hurt Sadie. She hadn't done anything to him.

Overcome with sadness, Boscoe laid down on the floor and let out a small whine.

At the mention of his name, Eva looked up at Jennifer, her mouth agape, and her eyes wide.

"It was Stephen Hill!"

"Stephen Hill? No, that's not possible. Why would he kill Sadie?"

"I think he might have been the one who killed Howard Smith, too. Remember Boscoe said someone was arguing with Howard? He heard it when Sadie let him out. That confirms what Sadie told Sarah about someone else being on Howard's porch. I think their argument got out of hand. Boscoe was barking, so Stephen must have heard it and saw Sadie waiting for Boscoe to come back in. He must have thought Sadie saw what had happened and killed her to make sure she didn't call the police."

"I doubt Sadie would have seen anything. Her vision wasn't good at night and Howard's house is set back from hers. I don't think she could have seen what was going on or who it was, even with the back floodlight on."

"It sounds like he didn't even ask before attacking Sadie. Boscoe told me something interesting we might be able to use as evidence, though. He said he bit Stephen on the arm before Stephen knocked him on the head. Do you remember Stephen had a bandage on his arm? I'm surprised it hasn't healed up by now, but maybe it got infected, or he didn't want anyone to see even a scab or a scar."

"Yes, I do remember, and something was off about him that night. I couldn't put my finger on it, but this would make sense as to why he was being so nosey. He must have wanted to see if we had any information that would implicate him."

"And we do! Remember the drops of blood that weren't Sadie's? That had to be his from when Boscoe bit him."

"I think you're right! But how do we prove it?" Jennifer asked, discouraged.

"I don't know, but let's tell the others about this at our next meeting. Between the four of us, maybe we'll think of something," Eva reassured her.

CHAPTER NINETEEN

*J*im is here.

"What? I wonder why he's here now?"

I assume that's a rhetorical question since he doesn't do his scheduling with me.

"Yes, it was rhetorical. Don't be a wise guy," she said as Jim knocked.

"Hi, did we have a date I forgot about?" Eva asked as she opened the door.

"No. I was passing by and decided to drop in. Is this a bad time?"

"Not at all. I'm just surprised to see you," she said, giving him a kiss on the cheek, hoping it would soften her question which came out in a brusquer tone than she intended.

"I was thinking about our trip to Camden and meaning it when I told you I'd like to see you more often. It came to me as I was getting close to your house, and I pulled into your driveway almost without thinking about it."

There was an awkward moment as they stood in the entry, neither one knowing what their next move should be before Eva regained her composure.

"I made some fresh lemonade. Would you like a glass? We can take it out to the sunroom. I've had the windows open, and the ceiling fan is on, so it's not too hot out there now."

"Sure, I'll take a glass. That sounds delicious."

Jim followed her into the kitchen with Reuben bringing up the rear.

Do you have any popcorn? This could get interesting.

Eva turned around to scowl at him, making Jim turn to see what she was looking at and only seeing Reuben. He raised his eyebrows at Eva, who realized too late she was reacting to Reuben's comment in a way she would usually only have done if they had been alone.

"That cat has been following me around all day," she said, trying to recover gracefully. "I love him, but sometimes he can be a pest."

"I guess that makes two of us who want to be with you, doesn't it, buddy?" he said, reaching down to scratch Reuben's chin, eliciting an appreciative purr.

Eva gave him an eyeroll as she got the pitcher of lemonade from the refrigerator and poured them each a tall glass before handing one to Jim.

"Your gardens really are lovely," Jim said as he took a seat in one of the Adirondack chairs which faced out to Eva's back yard.

"Thanks. I love being out in them, even the weeding. It helps me relax."

"Another reason I stopped by was to give you an update on the murders since you'd asked about them the other day. I know I should have called, but since I was in the neighborhood..."

"It's okay. I'm glad you stopped," Eva interrupted to reassure him.

"My buddies and I were talking about it at the police league softball game last night and they mentioned they've been following up with recent drug-related break-ins in some of the surrounding towns. None of those resulted in murders, but there's still the possibility it started as a break in that went south. I think they're trying to follow up even if it appears to be unrelated, in case it might give them a lead to a suspect or suspects. They still aren't sure if it was just one person."

"They don't actually have anyone in mind, though?" Eva asked.

"No, but they haven't given up either. I guess that's the part I wanted you to know. It must be worrisome the murderer hasn't been caught, but it still reads more like a random act, not an escalation in behavior."

"I appreciate that. It was upsetting when it first happened, but I've calmed down since then. There hasn't been anything to make me think I'm in any danger. I've been more worried about Jennifer and her family, though, since she lives right across the street. She did say Stephen Hill has been acting out of character lately. He's seemed nervous, which I guess is possible if he's worried about someone coming back and breaking into his house."

"That makes sense," Jim agreed.

Eva didn't want to push that line of discussion too much. She still hadn't figured out how to tell Jim about Boscoe telling her and Jennifer it was Stephen Hill who was the murderer. She was going to have to come up with something soon, though.

It was getting close to dinnertime and Jim wasn't making any moves toward leaving.

"Would you like to stay for dinner?" Eva asked. She had a salmon filet which would feed them both already in the fridge. She had planned to eat half of it that night and save the leftovers for a salad the next day but could always find something different for lunch.

"Sure, that would be nice."

"In that case, I should get started."

Jim followed her into the kitchen and sat at the bar in the

island, helping out by chopping the vegetables for the salad to go with the salmon and rice pilaf Eva was cooking.

"I miss this," Jim said, the sadness in his voice coming through.

"With your wife, you mean?"

"Yeah, I didn't do it as often as I probably should have. I don't want to make the same mistake with you."

Maybe it wasn't your imagination, Eva thought. She felt her emotional resistance kicking in, but cautioned herself to breathe and see where this was heading.

"You know I don't mind doing the cooking and I'll always ask if I need help. You don't ever have to feel guilty about not helping more."

"I know. It's not just the physical part of helping out I'm talking about, though. There's something about doing those sorts of things together that makes a couple more of a couple. I'm not sure if I'm explaining that well."

"You're doing fine. I understand what you mean, even though my ex and I never had that kind of relationship. Which, when I think about it, should have been a red flag, but it didn't come into my conscious awareness. After a while, I resented not only did he not help, but he didn't even offer to. I should have dealt with it, but I realized too late he wasn't the type to offer to do what he considered women's work and wasn't ever going to change. It wasn't something which had come up while we were dating. Part of that love is blind thing, I guess, and we didn't live together until after we were married. There's a lot you don't learn about someone until you're with them 24/7. I haven't felt that way with you, though. And I don't want to," she added.

"Good. I like you a lot, Eva, and I want us to be open and honest with each other. You let me know if I'm doing...or *not* doing...something that upsets you."

"I will," she promised. "Now, before this becomes too much like a Hallmark channel movie, let's eat."

They turned their conversation to less emotionally charged topics through their dinner and then moved to the living room to watch TV. Eva made the popcorn Reuben had asked about earlier, but for very different reasons. Eva sat on one end of the couch and Jim on the other, with Reuben stretched out between them while they watched a movie.

"Thanks for the dinner and a movie, and most of all, the company," Jim said after the movie was over. "I guess I should head home. It's getting late."

Despite his announcement, Eva sensed his reluctance to leave.

"Would you like to stay over?"

Jim considered. "I would, but I don't have any clothes or a toothbrush here and if there's one thing I can't tolerate, it's not brushing my teeth in the morning. Well, maybe two things. I don't like putting on dirty clothes either."

"Well, next time then. Bring your overnight bag."

Jim leaned over and gave Eva a kiss. When Eva opened her eyes, she knew from Jim's expression he was having an internal debate about whether to say more, but in the end, he rose from the couch and walked to the door, with Eva following.

"Good night," he said, leaning down to give her another kiss before leaving.

"I think I should have told him to bring some clothes and at least a toothbrush to leave here. What do you think?"

Why are you asking me?

"Well, this is your house, too. If Jim spends more time here, it will affect you as well."

That's true, but what's the real issue?

"You know me too well," she said, scowling, but not with anger. "I really like Jim, but I don't want to lose my freedom. I made that mistake before."

Think about what the pros and cons are.

Eva thought for several minutes before speaking again. "The

pro would be I'd have the opportunity to find out more about what it's like to be around Jim for longer stretches of time. I didn't do that with Kenneth, and it did not turn out well. The con would be that if we aren't able to be around each other, it could end the relationship."

That's true, Reuben agreed. *But is there a reason why you couldn't go back to the way it was? If you set the ground rules first, you both know where you stand.*

"You're right. I was thinking of it in either-or terms, but we're both adults and talking about it first would set our expectations of the outcome. It would be on a trial basis and see how it turns out. You're a genius, Reuben."

Well, duh.

"You don't have to be so smug," Eva said, annoyed at first, but knew he had been right, at least about not making it an all-or-nothing test.

Confident now about how to present her suggestion to Jim, she locked up the house for the night and headed to bed.

CHAPTER TWENTY

*D*etermined to present her idea to Jim, but nervous about his reaction, Eva called him the next morning.

"I have a proposition for you."

"I knew this was going to be a good day as soon as I woke up. Being propositioned by a beautiful woman confirmed it," Jim teased.

"We'll see how you feel after I tell you my idea," Eva cautioned. "I was thinking about your comment last night about not having any clothes or a toothbrush here. How would you feel about trying it out on a trial basis? We can take it slow and do more sleepovers, but if we decide it isn't working, we back it up. The last thing I want is for us to break up. It wasn't just Kenneth's refusal to help me out with chores around the house that caused our divorce. We'd both lived on our own for a long time before we got married. Maybe too long because we found out we didn't want to be around someone else full-time. My biggest worry is you and I would have the same problem."

Jim was silent for what seemed like a very long time and Eva was afraid she'd blown it, but at last he spoke.

"I don't want us to break up, either. I admit I'm hoping for more but for now, I can see how taking it slower has its benefits. As long as you're sure about this, how about if I bring over a toothbrush and enough clothes to stay over two nights instead of one? We'll see how it goes and either back it up or see if we can do longer stretches together."

Eva let out her breath. "That sounds great. I was so worried about how you'd react."

"I knew it was going to be a good day, and you proved me right."

"In that case, it sounds like we have a deal. I'll clean out a drawer for you, so you'll have a place to put your clothes the next time you come over."

"And in the spirit of taking things slowly, I won't ask if that's today," he teased.

As soon as they'd disconnected, Eva went to her bureau to make room for Jim's clothes, scanning her body for any sign she was going to regret the offer. She didn't feel any warning signs of tension.

"Let's hope this works!" she said aloud and felt a sense of optimism it would be a good thing.

CHAPTER TWENTY-ONE

*E*va was still pondering the dilemma of how to discuss Boscoe's revelation with Jim, but no closer to a solution. She had never told him about her ability to communicate with animals, but was considering taking the leap of faith. This information was too important to withhold because she was afraid he would think she was a kook. She would have to find the way to tell him without scaring him away or having him think she was pulling his leg. But how?

Careful. If you think any harder, you're going to have steam coming out of your ears, Reuben's comment interrupted her thoughts.

"Hilarious."

What's got you so riled up?

"A couple days ago I went to Jennifer's to talk to Sadie Emerson's dog, Boscoe. We were hoping he could tell us who her killer was."

And did he?

"Yes, he did. But now we need to figure out how to get that information to the authorities in a way they'll believe us. I can't exactly tell them her dog told me."

That is a problem. Too bad all humans don't have your ability to understand animals. We have so much to say, but they ignore us.

"It's not that we're ignoring you. We just don't speak your language. And, unfortunately, there are no apps to teach us or translate for us. I've been debating whether to tell Jim what I learned from Boscoe but haven't figured out how to do it without having him run for the hills, thinking I've gone off the deep end."

That would be too bad. I actually like Jim, and you know I'm particular about which humans I can tolerate.

"Why, Reuben, I didn't realize you cared that much about Jim. Now I really don't want to say anything to make him leave, never to come back. Any suggestions?"

Let me sleep on it. I was about to take a cat nap anyway, no pun intended.

Reuben gave her a side eye, almost daring her to make a comment as he walked toward the window seat in the living room's bay window, but Eva held her tongue.

A half hour later, Reuben padded into Eva's sewing room, sat down near her sewing machine, and began washing his front left paw. It was his way of letting her know he wanted her attention but making her be the one to initiate the conversation.

"What's new, pussycat?" she asked.

Reuben stopped in mid-lick and looked up at Eva, his eyes narrowed in disgust.

I don't believe you said that!

"Just be glad I didn't add whoa, whoa, whoa, whoa."

I'm about to walk back out of the room without telling you my idea, Reuben said testily.

"My apologies. What did you come up with?"

The problem Jim will have is thinking you're imagining you're speaking to animals. But what if you can prove it by having me tell you what he's thinking and you repeating it to him?

"It would have to be something I couldn't just guess, though," Eva said, thinking over likely scenarios. "I'd have to ask him to think of something he's never told me and I wouldn't have known some other way." Eva's excitement grew as she considered the possibility this could work.

Exactly!

"Thanks, Reuben! You're smarter than the average bear."

I would hope so, Reuben said, getting up and walking back to his cushion on the window seat before Eva had the chance to make any more ridiculous comments. To further emphasize his annoyance, his tail was switching back and forth. She saw it, but rather than being chastised, she chuckled quietly and knew he'd heard when she saw one of his ears twitch.

Excited to put their plan into action, Eva called Jim.

"How would you like to come for dinner and a sleepover? I've even emptied a drawer for you to leave some clothes. I have something I want to share with you, and I'm hoping you'll have an open mind."

"Ummm… okay. That doesn't sound ominous at all."

"I guess that did come out a bit dramatically. It's not something I want to talk about over the phone, though. I'll need you here in person to explain it properly."

"That clears it all up," Jim said, but Eva could hear the humor in his voice.

"Well, can you come?"

"How can I say no? You've got my interest piqued. What time?"

"Does five-thirty work? And don't forget to bring some extra clothes to leave."

"Yes, ma'am. Can't wait!"

CHAPTER TWENTY-TWO

*E*va tried to hide her nervousness when Jim arrived for dinner. She was hopeful a good meal and either a couple bottles of beer or glasses of wine would loosen things up enough that Jim would be more receptive to her revelation she had conversations with animals.

"Something smells good," Jim said as he let himself in and walked into the kitchen. He held up a small duffel bag. "I brought my extra clothes. If you can show me where I should put them, I'll get them out of the way."

"As a matter of fact, I can. Follow me."

After putting the clothes in the designated drawer and his toothbrush in the bathroom, they walked back to the kitchen.

"We haven't had lasagna for a while, so I cooked up a batch and made the sauce from scratch. You're welcome to help yourself to the leftovers if you want to take some home with you tomorrow. I'll put in some salad and garlic bread, too. Can I get you a glass of wine to start out while the lasagna finishes cooking, or maybe a beer?"

"What are you drinking?"

"I'm going to have a glass of wine."

"That's what I'll have, too, then. Do you need it opened?"

Eva handed him the bottle of wine and a corkscrew and put out two wine glasses, which Jim filled and put on the table to breathe while Eva finished up her cooking duties. The oven timer went off, and she pulled out the lasagna, which she placed on the counter and replaced it with a loaf of garlic bread.

"That should be done in about ten to fifteen minutes, but we can start with the salad."

She took the salad out of the refrigerator and put it on the dining room table, which she'd set earlier and decorated with a bouquet of flowers picked from her garden. She'd considered lighting a candle, but thought it might be too much. A romantic evening wasn't her primary purpose for the dinner, and she didn't want to give Jim the wrong impression.

"This looks really nice, Eva," Jim said as he looked at the tableau she had arranged. "Did I forget it's our anniversary?" he asked, teasing, but Eva knew he was only half-kidding.

"No, no, don't get yourself all worried. I do have that thing I want to talk to you about, but let's enjoy our wine and dinner."

"It still sounds serious. *Should* I be worried?"

"Let's hope not. I am a little nervous about how to bring it up and I'm hoping you won't go running for the hills after you've heard what I have to tell you. I might have information about Sadie Emerson's murder."

Jim looked up from his salad in surprise at Eva's announcement.

"Really? How did you hear about it?"

"Well, that's what I'm nervous about. How I got the information is, well... unorthodox might be the way to describe it." She took a sip of her wine, both to give herself time to think about what she wanted to say next and some liquid courage.

Jim waited patiently for her to continue. Realizing she would not be able to put it off until they'd finished dinner, she took a deep breath and began.

"When I was a little girl, I discovered I had an ability that no one else around me did. I thought everyone could do this, but I learned that adults thought I had an overactive imagination and other children thought I was weird, so I hid it. My parents thought I'd outgrown it and I had realized I was being silly when I stopped sharing with them. I've never spoken about this with anyone else until just recently with my quilt club group. Not even my ex-husband knew about it."

The timer went off again and Eva was grateful for the interruption to calm her nerves while she dished out the lasagna and sliced the garlic bread. Jim was still silent, but she didn't sense he was upset, just curious.

"Why don't we eat our meal first and I'll finish up with my story when we're done. Tell me about your day," she said, to give them something else to talk about.

Jim raised his eyebrows but took the hint and told her about his day instead of pushing her to finish.

"That was delicious. I hope you'll have enough to give me a big slice to take home and I'll take some salad and garlic bread, too, since you offered. Would you like another glass of wine?" he asked, holding up the bottle and then refilling both their glasses when she nodded yes.

"Let's clear up the kitchen and take the wine into the living room where we can relax before I finish my true confessions."

Eva retrieved plastic containers from her pantry for Jim's slice of lasagna, salad, and bread and after the dishes were loaded in the dishwasher and leftover food stored in the refrigerator, they made their way to the living room with their wineglasses and what was left in the bottle of wine.

"So, what is this dark secret you've been hiding all these years?"

"First, I'm fully aware this is going to take a huge leap of faith on your part to believe me or, if you don't, to not have me committed after you hear it. I'm hoping I can prove what I tell you is real, though."

"I'll try to keep an open mind," Jim said, facing her on the couch.

Is this my cue?

"Yes, Reuben, this is your cue," Eva replied.

Jim did a double take when he saw Reuben hop down from his cushion in the bay window and walk over to the couch, jumping up to sit between them. Jim reached out to scratch his head, and Reuben purred appreciatively.

"My ability, or I prefer to think of it as a gift, is that I can communicate with animals."

Jim's face cracked in a wide grin. "You really had me going there, Eva."

"I'm serious," Eva replied, and the smile on Jim's face was replaced with a look of doubt.

"I thought everyone talked to animals. These days, I do it telepathically when other people are around instead of out loud. I realize this is going to be a lot for you to take in or believe, so Reuben and I came up with an idea for how to prove it. I want you to think of something you've never told me, and better yet, something you haven't told anyone else, and Reuben will communicate it to me. Then I'll tell you what he's said. Do you think that would be enough to convince you I'm not pulling your leg and it's not some kind of parlor trick I'm trying to play on you?"

Jim thought this over. "I honestly don't know how to answer that. A part of me can see the logic of how it would work, but the bigger part of me is thinking it's totally nuts."

"That's fair. Are you willing to give it a try, though?"

"Well, I guess it wouldn't hurt to humor you… and Reuben," he added, smiling at the cat and scratching under his chin.

If this didn't feel so good, I'd be walking back to my cushion after that remark.

Eva chose to let that go in the interest of moving the experiment along.

"Okay, is there something you can think of you haven't told me or I wouldn't have heard from someone else?"

Jim sat deep in thought and then smiled.

"I think I've got it."

"Okay. While you tell Reuben what it is, I'm going to go out to the sunroom. Is that far enough away that you won't think I was able to hear you?"

"I guess it should be."

"Give me a shout when you're done, and I'll come back."

Reuben sat up and gave Jim his full attention. Jim felt ridiculous but he'd agreed to do this, so he told Reuben his secret and then called to Eva that it was okay to return.

He was thinking about when he was a little boy and he hid a jar of pennies under a loose floorboard in his bedroom, he told her once she had come back.

"Reuben told me you were thinking about the jar of pennies you hid under a floorboard in your bedroom when you were a little boy."

Jim's eyes grew round, and his mouth dropped.

"How…"

"Would you like to think of something else just to make sure that wasn't a fluke?" Eva asked. When he agreed, she walked back to the sunroom. After a few minutes, she heard Jim calling to her.

"This time he said you were thinking about the time you went for a joyride in your mother's car in the middle of the night to do doughnuts after a snowstorm," Eva said.

His mouth didn't drop open this time, but Jim's eyes were just as round, and he looked down at Reuben and then back at Eva before shaking his head as though to clear his thoughts.

"I don't know how you did that, but it's exactly what I was thinking both times."

"It's important you believe me because what I have to tell you about Sadie's murder depends on it."

"I don't think I have any choice but to believe you. I've never told anyone else about either of those things, and I'm positive I didn't say it loud enough to hear unless you've got super hearing powers." He hesitated a few seconds before continuing. "And you got that from Reuben, not reading my mind yourself?"

"No, I can't read minds. And it's not really reading their minds in the way you mean it. We're communicating telepathically. I never intrude when we're not having a conversation. That would just be wrong."

Jim laughed at the idea of there being telepathy etiquette between humans and animals, and Eva joined in, realizing how it must sound.

"Okay, I guess I'm a believer and now this explains a lot about the looks you two would give each other sometimes. I thought I was imagining it, but it was real. You must have been doing your telepathy thing. How does this fit into Sadie Emerson's murder, though? Reuben wasn't involved with that, was he?"

Reuben turned his head to look at Jim, his own eyes round now, and then hopped off the couch. *I can't believe he would say that!*

"I think you hurt his feelings. That wasn't meant as an accusation, was it?"

"Oh, no, of course not! Sorry, buddy, that came out wrong."

Reuben ignored him and jumped up onto his cushion, settling in with his back turned to Jim.

"It wasn't Reuben who told me who killed Sadie. It was her dog, Boscoe."

"Her dog?"

"Yes. Jennifer had let us into Sadie's house last week so Sarah... from my quilting club... could try to make contact with

Sadie, which she did, but just as she was about to tell Sarah who her killer was…"

"Wait a minute. Back up the bus. Your friend Sarah was trying to communicate with Sadie's ghost?"

"Oh, right. You didn't know that part before, either. Maybe I should start at the beginning with the first meeting of our quilting club," Eva said, as she became fully aware of Jim's somewhat shell-shocked expression. "Okay, bear with me. This is going to be a *lot* to take in and accept. I hadn't planned to dump this all on you tonight… or maybe ever… but it just slipped out. And now I'm afraid that even after our demonstration with Reuben, this might be more than you can accept."

"I confess I heard a lot of stories in my time as a state trooper and some of them were pretty wild, but I always tried to keep an open mind. Sometimes, the wildest stories turned out to be the ones that actually turned out to be true. I'm going to give you the same benefit of the doubt."

Eva took a moment to search Jim's face for any sign he was only humoring her.

He's telling you the truth. He's willing to let you explain.

Eva looked over at Reuben, who had turned to face them so he could watch the show taking place between Jim and Eva. Her confidence returning, she took a deep breath and resumed her recounting of the first meeting of the Cozy Quilts Club.

"None of us realized we each had special abilities until our first quilt club meeting. Annalise was the one who discovered it. In addition to being a Reiki practitioner, she has psychic abilities, and she tuned into each of us. As I said, Sarah can communicate with ghosts…"

"Like that kid in *The Sixth Sense*?"

"Exactly!" Eva confirmed. "And Jennifer has the ability to do psychometry."

"What's that?"

"It's when someone is able to get impressions or images

about the person who owned the article she's touching. Usually it's something they've worn, like a piece of jewelry or clothing. She hasn't had anything like that happen yet about Sadie, but now that I think about it..." Eva paused, thinking aloud, "maybe we can try that, too. I'll have to mention it to her."

"So going back, you were at Sadie's house with Sarah, and she was communicating with Sadie," Jim encouraged her back on track.

"Oh, right, sorry, I got distracted. All of the club members were there, so we all witnessed what happened. Sadie was about to tell Sarah who killed her when there was a knock at the door. It was Stephen Hill. He lives beside Sadie on one side and Howard Smith, the guy they found who was murdered, too, lives on the other side. He claimed he wanted to make sure nothing was wrong because of all the cars in the driveway. We all thought he was acting more nosey than concerned, and Jennifer thought something was off about how he was acting."

"Off?"

"She couldn't put her finger specifically on what felt odd, but it was a gut feeling."

"It was nagging at the back of my mind, too, and I got the idea to ask Jennifer if I could talk to Boscoe since he was with Sadie when it happened. She thought it was a great idea, so we set up a meeting. The first time we met at Jennifer's house but Boscoe still hadn't fully recovered from his head injury and couldn't remember everything that happened to him and Sadie. She called two days later to say he was doing much better and asked me to come back to try again. I went over that afternoon, and we went to Sadie's house with Boscoe. This time it was just the two, well three of us counting Boscoe, and I parked at Jennifer's house so there were no strange cars in Sadie's driveway. Boscoe had already told me what he could remember about that night, including that he had heard someone arguing with Howard Smith just before Sadie called him in for the night. They were about to go to bed when someone knocked at their door. Sadie peeked out the window and recognized who it was, so let him in. That's where he had his lapse of memory the first time I talked to him. The next time, though, he remembered it was Stephen Hill."

"*Stephen Hill?*" Jim asked incredulously. "That can't be possible. Why would he want to kill Sadie?"

"We think he was trying to cover his tracks. We also think he is the one who killed Howard Smith, too, and he thought Sadie must have seen him when Boscoe was outside barking."

Jim considered that piece of information.

"But there's something else Boscoe told me that could be of vital importance. He said when Stephen attacked Sadie, he bit him on his arm, and he had a bandage on that arm the night when he interrupted Sarah. Stephen hit Boscoe with the same weapon he'd used to kill Sadie and knocked him unconscious, so he didn't see Stephen leave. The important piece about this is that bite. It makes sense to me that the drops of blood the crime scene unit found must be his. Also, he said the weapon was a long piece of metal with a hook on one end and a notch on the other. He didn't know the word for it, but it sounds like it might have been a crowbar to me."

Jim remained quiet, taking this all in.

"I hadn't told you the medical examiner determined a crowbar was most likely what had been used, had I?"

"No you hadn't told me that."

If Jim hadn't believed Eva's story before, it seemed he did now.

"The obvious problem with all of this is that the police aren't likely to arrest Stephen Hill on the word of Boscoe's testimony," Eva said.

"So, the question is, how do we get him to confess?" Jim agreed.

"Yes! I'm guessing there's also no way to force him to submit his DNA to prove the blood found at the scene was his."

"No, they don't have probable cause."

"So, I guess that means we're still back to square one of bringing Sadie and Howard's killer to justice."

"For now, at least. Killers usually slip up, though, and make a mistake that gives the cops what they need to make an arrest and get a confession."

"I hope so. Stephen appears to be a nice guy and I'm hoping this was a horrible lack of judgement on his part brought on by the panic of the moment. If he killed Howard first because they were arguing, he was already in a bad place, and killing Sadie was caused by fear of getting caught for Howard's murder. Still, she didn't deserve that, and I won't be sorry if… no, *when*… he's finally arrested and goes to jail."

There wasn't any more they could do that night, but they both agreed they would keep thinking about possible ways to bring the police's attention to Stephen.

CHAPTER TWENTY-THREE

"Now who can that be?" Eva said aloud, slightly annoyed by the interruption to her sewing when she heard her cell phone's ringer. She had been absorbed in a project which had been on her to do list for some time. Making the crumb quilt pieces had spurred her to action, and she was now cutting the larger pieces of leftover scraps into uniform quilting block sizes she would be able to choose from later to make a scrappy quilt. This is the name quilters use to describe quilts made from random colors and print designs of fabric rather than a planned color theme, the result being very colorful quilts. It was especially satisfying to Eva's sensibility of not wasting fabric. She knew some people discarded the leftover scraps after they'd made a project, but that wasn't her style even before the focus on recycling and repurposing became popular again. Although she'd put a dent in it after making the crumb pieces, her large bin of scraps from past projects was still overflowing, and it was time to do something about it. She had finished sorting the pieces into similar colors and ironed them so they could be cut into the various sizes when the phone had rung.

"Hello," she said, trying to keep the annoyance out of her voice.

"Hi, Eva. It's Annalise. Did I call at a bad time?"

"Not a bad time exactly. I was trying to organize my fabric stash and was about to start cutting, but I can take a break."

"Oh, I'm so sorry. Should I call back later? I was going to ask if you'd like to meet for lunch, but if you're busy…"

"That's okay. I think I will be done by lunchtime. We could go to The Checkout Diner if that works for you. If you come here first, though, I'll show you what I'm working on, and we can chat privately so I can share with you the information I learned from Boscoe."

"What you learned from Boscoe?"

"Oh, that's right. Jennifer and I agreed to wait until we saw everyone in person to share this, so I haven't told you or Sarah. We took Boscoe to Sadie's house, and he was able to tell me what happened. I'll fill in the gaps when you get here."

"That would be wonderful. I don't have any appointments this afternoon, so we wouldn't be rushed. Should I come by around twelve-thirty?"

"That's perfect. I'll see you then!"

* * *

THREE STACKS of fabric were neatly lined up on Eva's cutting table as her bin of leftover fabrics were transformed into five-inch, three-inch and two-and-a-half inch squares perfect for future quilt projects. Although not quite finished with the cutting, she stopped shortly before noon so she would have time to get ready for Annalise's arrival. Reuben, who had been occupying his usual spot in the bay window, padded into the sewing room.

Are you finally done? he asked, and his expression clearly told her he was annoyed by the lack of attention she'd been giving him.

"Not yet, Reuben. Do you think you're being neglected?"

That would be assuming I enjoyed your company.

"Oh, now, don't go pretending you don't. You know you'd miss me if I wasn't around."

I'd miss being fed.

"Speaking of which, I'd better change before Annalise gets here. I don't want to go out in public in these old clothes," Eva said, heading to the bedroom with Reuben trailing behind.

She's the one who dresses like a hippie? Reuben asked.

"And how would you know how a hippie dresses? That was more than a little before your time."

I've seen the documentaries on television. I pay more attention than you think I do.

"I guess you do, but we don't call anyone a hippie these days. I believe that style of fashion is called Bohemian or BOHO for short, and personally, I like it."

I don't see you wearing it.

"Well, that's because I don't think I could pull it off with the same sense of panache that Annalise does," Eva replied, as she selected a pair of black shorts and a flowered blouse from her walk-in closet along with a pair of sandals.

Bored with Eva's activities, Reuben gave his body a generous stretch and returned to the living room, hopping up to the bay window to keep watch for Annalise. The living room had a couch and two very comfortable chairs Reuben would occasionally lie on, mostly when Eva was there, so she would be close enough to stroke his fur and scratch under his chin and ears. But he considered the cushion in the bay window to be his throne where he could survey his domain, both indoors and out.

She's here, he announced as Eva walked into the living room.

"Thanks, Reuben. I don't know why I bothered with a doorbell when I've got you here."

Maybe you're the one who'd be missing someone instead of the other way around, Reuben replied haughtily.

"You know I would," Eva said with genuine affection in her voice.

Eva opened the door to find Annalise on her doorstep, finger poised in mid-air above the doorbell.

"Reuben told me you were here," Eva said, smiling as Annalise withdrew her finger.

Annalise smiled in return as she looked in Reuben's direction to see him sitting facing them, but not making any move to join the festivities.

"Thanks, Reuben," Annalise offered, but no acknowledgement was forthcoming.

"Would you rather go to lunch first and come back here after?"

"I'm hungry, but I'm more interested in hearing all about your conversation with Boscoe."

"Let's go into the living room then where it's more comfortable."

"Your living room is so cozy," Annalise said as she looked around the room. The paint on the walls was a soft yellow and the sofa and two chairs were a neutral beige, but multi-colored floral cushions were scattered on them to add pops of color. The sofa was on one side of a coffee table facing the wall on which the TV was mounted, and on the other were the chairs facing toward the sofa, encouraging a conversational atmosphere. A soft green afghan which was obviously hand knit was draped on the back and arm of one chair as elegantly as you would see in any magazine picture. The space under the furniture was covered with a floral rug in pale shades of blue, beige, and green complementing the medium brown hardwood floors. A row of tall bookcases filled with books and knickknacks she'd collected over the years stood against the wall dividing the living room from Eva's bedroom. The sunlight coming in through the windows added to the warmth both literally and figuratively.

"Thank you so much. I hear that a lot, so I must have done something right, although I can't say it was planned," Eva said self-consciously.

"You must have trusted your intuition," Annalise told her with a smile.

"Can I get you something to drink? I have the coffee on, but I can make tea, or I've got cold drinks available, too," Eva offered.

"A glass of water would be great for now and I'll wait until after lunch for the coffee. Do you need help with anything?"

"No, no. I'm all set. You make yourself comfortable and I'll be right back with the drinks."

Eva returned with a glass of water in each hand, setting one down for Annalise on the coffee table and then sitting down in her usual spot on the couch, placing her drink on a coaster on the end table beside her.

"I've been hardly able to contain myself. I've been so excited to hear all about your meeting with Boscoe," Annalise said as she picked up her glass of water.

"I don't know why I didn't think to ask Jennifer earlier, but I'm so glad it finally occurred to me after Sarah was interrupted. We had to try twice because the first time Boscoe couldn't remember everything that happened. A couple of days later, Jennifer called to tell me he was back to himself and asked if I would try again. Once I got to her house, she suggested we try at Sadie's house, so we walked over. It's possible someone saw us going into the house, but at least no strange cars were parked in the driveway to attract attention like the last time."

"Smart," Annalise said, nodding her head in approval.

"I feel so bad for Boscoe. He's adjusting to being with Jennifer's family, but he's still so lost without Sadie."

"It's good he's got someone he already knew to take him in. That should help," Annalise said.

"I think so, too," Eva agreed. She paused to gather her thoughts before continuing with her recitation of what happened next.

"Boscoe told us he had seen two people on Howard Smith's front porch who appeared to be arguing. He had barked, trying to alert Sadie to what was going on, but she wanted him to come back inside, which he did. They were getting ready to go to bed when someone knocked at the front door. At first, Sadie wasn't going to answer, but they knocked again. Sadie looked outside before opening the door. She recognized who was standing there, so she let him in. Almost as soon as he was inside and she'd shut the door, that's when he hit her on the head with what Boscoe could only describe as a long piece of metal. Jennifer and I think he must have meant a crowbar, and Jim confirmed it when I told him."

"You told Jim you'd talked to Boscoe? Annalise asked incredulously.

"Oh, right, I haven't told you about that either, but that's another story and I'll get to it in a minute. As soon as Sadie fell to the floor, Boscoe bit her attacker on the arm but he got hit on the head as well and when he woke up, the man was gone, and Sadie was dead. He stayed right by her side all night until Jennifer found them the next morning. But the important part is he was able to tell us who the attacker was. It was Stephen Hill."

Annalise gasped.

"No wonder he was nosing around the night we were there!" she exclaimed. "I thought something was off about him, but it wasn't coming through clearly. We were all trying to hide our true intentions for being there if he got past Jennifer, so I think it was muddying the waters."

"The problem now is, what can we do about it? It's one thing that we know who Sadie's killer is, but the police aren't going to believe us. Without any physical evidence connecting him to the crime scene, they don't have any reason to suspect he's involved."

"It's not likely he's going to confess, either," Annalise agreed.

They sat in silence, each lost in their own thoughts about their dilemma.

Why don't you just tell him you know what he did? He may be feeling guilty but thinking he can get away with it if nobody knows, Reuben offered.

"But how do we let him know that we know he did it?" Eva asked aloud.

"What's happening?" Annalise asked.

"Oh, I'm sorry. I forgot you can't hear Reuben. He's asking why we don't tell Stephen Hill we know he did it and maybe he'll feel so guilty he'll confess."

They both fell silent again, considering this.

"It might work," Annalise said after several minutes, more to herself than Eva and then looked directly at Eva. "What if we call a meeting of the Cozy Quilts Club to discuss it and make sure the others are on board, but here's my idea. We come up with some excuse to invite Stephen Hill to Sadie's house, where we confront him with what you and Sarah learned from Sadie and Boscoe. In the meantime, I'll see if I can connect telepathically and find out where he hid the murder weapon…"

"We wouldn't want to tip him off about that, though, in case he got rid of it before the police obtain a search warrant."

"Oh, right. Good point," Annalise said. "But we could record everything using our phone's voice memo app, so we'd have his confession on tape… or whatever it is you call it with a phone."

"I think they say digitally. And that would be assuming he does confess."

"You know, I think he will," Annalise said, smiling.

"Fingers crossed."

"Don't forget to tell me about how you told Jim you can communicate with animals."

"Oh, right! I realized the only way I could tell him Stephen Hill is the killer is by telling him how I got the information. It was Reuben who came up with the idea of how to do that and have Jim believe me. He suggested Jim tell him something he'd never told anyone before, then he told me what it was and I repeated it back to Jim. I wasn't sure I'd be able to do it because I didn't want to jeopardize my relationship with Jim. In the end, though, I realized I would have to trust he would believe me because there might be no other way to bring Stephen Hill to justice."

"How did Jim react?"

Eva chuckled. "I wish you could have seen his face! I'm convinced he thought I was pulling his leg, but when Reuben told me what he was thinking and I repeated it, his chin nearly fell to the floor. To reinforce it wasn't a lucky guess, I had Jim do another experiment. When Reuben repeated that one as well, he became a believer. Or at least less of a skeptic. And best of all, he didn't hightail it out of here, never to return."

Annalise laughed. "That's fantastic news. I'm happy for you, Eva. Being able to share that with him and have him accept it, and you, is a real show of trust for both of you."

"That's how I feel, too. It's such a relief to have him accept me as I am and not feel judged. It's how I feel with all of you in the Cozy Quilts Club. Like I've finally found my people, if you know what I mean."

"I do indeed."

Here we go again with your kumbaya moments, Reuben interjected, breaking the mood for Eva. She mimicked one of his expressions by narrowing her eyes and glaring at him.

"I assume that look isn't because of anything I said."

"No, Annalise. Reuben was being snarky. I'm not going to repeat what he said."

Annalise chuckled. "You wouldn't hurt my feelings. Back to Jim, though. Do you think he will help us if we can get Stephen to confess, even after finding out our methods are pretty unconventional?"

"I do, or at least more so than I would have if he didn't believe me about Boscoe telling me he's the killer."

"Good! We're going to need him on our side if we're going to convince the police they should follow up on what we learn."

"I agree and now we just need to convince Jennifer and Sarah your plan will work. That settled, let me show you what I've been up to this morning and then how about we go for lunch? I'm starving."

"Me, too."

CHAPTER TWENTY-FOUR

They drove separately so Annalise could go directly home once they were finished with their lunch, but only two other cars were in the parking lot. *That had to be the convenience store where Stephen Hill had come the night of Howard and Sadie's murders,* Eva was thinking as she pulled into a parking spot. She wondered if the store had any security cameras that would have captured him on video to corroborate the story he had told Jennifer. She made a mental note to herself to check for either signage or the camera itself after she and Annalise had finished their lunch. Jim hadn't mentioned anything about Stephen Hill's statement of being there as having been confirmed by the detectives investigating the murders. It was possible he might not have that piece of information or have told her even if he had. She'd have to ask him later. Since Stephen was the last one to have seen Howard Smith alive before his murder, she assumed they must have wanted to check his alibi about being at the convenience store at the time it happened.

"Hello, ladies," the diner's waitress, Betty Jones, called out from behind the counter.

"Hello, Betty. Should we just pick a booth?" Eva asked.

"Sure. No reservations are needed here," she said with a smile handing them each a menu as they passed by.

Annalise and Eva walked to the end of the row of booths, picking one that would offer them some privacy. Annalise sat facing the door and caught her breath as soon as she'd sat down.

"Are you alright?" Eva asked.

Annalise nodded and whispered, looking down at her menu rather than directly at Eva. "Don't look around, but Stephen Hill is in the booth next to the door." Neither of them had noticed as they'd walked to their booth, as his back had been to them.

"Is he alone?" Eva asked, keeping her voice lowered.

"Yes. It looks like he's getting ready to leave," Annalise said, sneaking a peek at Stephen. As if on cue, he had picked up his check and walked to the cash register, where he handed the check and cash to Betty.

"Keep the change," he told her, and then walked out the door, leaving Annalise and Eva alone in the diner with Betty.

"Can I get you something to drink?" Betty asked, order pad in hand.

"Just water with lemon for me," Eva said.

"I'll have a raspberry lemonade if you have it," Annalise said.

"We do. I'll be right back with that and give you a minute to decide what you're having. The special today is a lobster roll with your choice of french fries, potato salad, or coleslaw."

"That sounds delicious. No need to look at the menu. I'll have that with the coleslaw," Annalise said.

"The same for me, but with french fries," Eva said, handing Betty her menu, and Annalise handed over hers as well.

"Coming right up," Betty said and walked back to the kitchen to put in the order.

Waiting until she was sure Betty was out of earshot, Eva said,

"I want to check out the convenience store when we're done to see if they have any security cameras."

"What for?" Annalise asked, a frown on her face.

"Do you remember Stephen told Jennifer he had been here at the time Howard Smith was murdered? I wonder if he told that to the police, too, and if they've confirmed it either by asking the clerk who was working that night or taking a look at the security tapes."

"Okay, but how would that matter?"

"Oh, well, maybe it wouldn't," she said, somewhat deflated. "I'll ask Jim if they have that information already, though. If we can get his confession, and his DNA matches the blood, it would put him at the scene of Sadie's murder, anyway. I guess I'm overcomplicating it or have watched too many murder mystery shows on TV," Eva said.

"Shhh, Betty's coming," Annalise said.

"Here you go, ladies," she said, placing their orders on the booth's table. "If you need anything else, let me know."

"Thanks, Betty. Say, have you heard any talk about the murders?" Annalise asked, feigning ignorance.

This made Betty's face light up with the prospect of sharing the local gossip.

"Isn't it something? Who would have thought in our little community we'd have TWO murders, let alone two murders in the same week?!"

"It's awful, isn't it?" Eva replied. "Not knowing who the killer is and they're still out there has had me on edge. I heard you told Deputy Tremblay about Greg Ellingwood but he had an alibi."

"That's what I heard, too, about the alibi that is."

"At least you gave them another possibility. Sometimes ruling out suspects is just as valuable."

"Stephen Hill was just in here... you might have seen him

when you first came in… he lives right next to Sadie and Howard's houses, you know."

Annalise and Eva both nodded their acknowledgement and Betty continued.

"He told me the police are stumped. They've questioned him because he's their neighbor, but he was here at the convenience store on the night Howard was killed at about the same time. Ricky was on duty that night and confirmed that Stephen was here when he said he was. Can you imagine the police would suspect him?!" Betty asked, her incredulous tone clearly indicating *she* couldn't, but carried on before waiting for a reply. "I heard they suspected Jennifer Ryder's cousin, Thomas Patterson, but he had an alibi, too. Everybody who's been talking about it thinks it must have been some random attack by a drug addict looking for pills, but things got out of hand. That doesn't ring true for me, though. Would they really kill two people just to steal drugs?"

"It doesn't make sense to me, either," Eva agreed.

"Well, I should let you ladies eat your lunch before those french fries get cold," she said and hurried off to wait on the couple who had entered the diner.

"Won't she be surprised?" Annalise said, keeping her voice low.

"Let's hope we'll be able to prove her wrong, at least about him," Eva said.

CHAPTER TWENTY-FIVE

*E*va was both excited and nervous about sharing the plan she and Annalise had worked out to trap Stephen Hill into a confession. She'd put off bringing it up during the potluck dinner portion of their meeting, but the time had come to discuss it with Jennifer and Sarah and hope they'd be on board.

"I need to bring you up to speed, Sarah. Annalise and Jennifer already know this, but I hadn't wanted to bother you before the meeting tonight because I know you've been so busy with your day job," she began. "Since our last meeting, your attempt to communicate with Sadie gave me the inspiration to try the same with Boscoe. I don't know why it took me so long to think of it, but it's a good thing I did. We had to try twice but the second time, Jennifer and I took him to his house, mostly because we'd have more privacy, but thought it might be helpful to have Boscoe in his old home to speak with him about the night Sadie was murdered. He told me some of the same things Sadie had told you, but the most important thing is he identified the killer. It was Stephen Hill."

Sarah's eyes grew round as she looked at the others, who were waiting to see her reaction.

"That's amazing!" she began, and then frowned. "But how do we prove it?"

"That's what I wanted to talk to you all about tonight. Annalise came up with the idea and I think it's a good one if we can work out the details. She suggested we find some excuse to have Stephen Hill come to the house. We'll all have our phones set to record the conversation and, with a lot of luck, we'll get him to confess. Do you remember I mentioned... although I shouldn't have... that the Evidence Response Team found a couple drops of blood that weren't Sadie's?"

They all nodded.

"If we can convince him to have a drink with us, we can take his glass to the police so they can check his DNA against the blood drops found at Sadie's. They wouldn't even need a warrant if the TV shows are being accurate about the legalities of using something the killer has voluntarily left his DNA on."

"But how do we convince the police to listen to us in the first place?" Sarah asked.

"I'll ask Jim to take Jennifer to the police station with the recording of Stephen Hill's confession along with the glass. They'd be more likely to listen to a retired law enforcement officer if he's backing us up."

"And how do you convince Jim to believe the information to implicate Stephen Hill in the first place, especially about how we got it?" Jennifer asked.

"It wasn't something I wanted to do because I was afraid he would think I'm crazy, but Reuben came up with an idea to demonstrate I can communicate with animals. I asked Jim to think of something he hadn't told anyone else, which he did, and then Reuben told me. After I'd told Jim what it was, and then Reuben did it one more time, he couldn't argue it was at least possible I can hear and understand what Reuben was saying. Then I told him about my talk with Boscoe and Sarah's session with Sadie. If he wasn't already sitting down, he could have been knocked over with a feather! I realize I probably shouldn't have said anything without your permission first, but it slipped out without my even thinking about it. It wasn't possible for me to tell him about what Sadie told Sarah without sharing the abilities each of you have, too. After what happened with Reuben, he's at least a believer in the possibility we each have these abilities and doesn't think we're kooks or charlatans. I haven't discussed with him the idea of getting Stephen to confess or getting his DNA, though. A big part of me was afraid he'd try to talk me out of it."

When she finished, everyone was quiet, but the excitement in the room was palpable.

"Do you really think this will work?" Jennifer asked.

"What do we have to lose?" Eva asked. "Other than Stephen Hill thinking we're a bunch of kooks? I doubt he'd repeat any of what we tell him, though, since he's the one being accused of the crime. I checked on the internet and then confirmed with Jim that in Maine it's a one party consent law for recording conversations without the other person's knowledge. Since we're all aware the recording is being done, we're covered, and it should be legal. As long as Stephen confesses, do we care if the police find out our methods for learning how he did it?" she asked, looking at each member of the group.

They all shook their heads.

"Jennifer, if you could make sure there's something for all of us to drink before we tell Stephen what we know, we can bag his glass to take to the police for processing. They don't always reveal to the public everything they've learned from a crime scene, so we may have to tell a white lie about why Jennifer is bringing in the glass. We don't want them to know that Jim, well really it was me, shared that they have the blood drops evidence. Maybe you can say you were thinking they might have collected DNA from the crime scene but don't have a suspect to match it with, so took his glass just in case," Eva suggested. "That, along with the confession, will at least make them think about looking more closely at him and, hopefully, a warrant for his arrest."

Smooth, she heard Reuben interject and looked down to see him sitting on the floor beside her nonchalantly licking his front paw. She bent down to scratch the top of his head but made no other reply.

"Sure, I can do that," Jennifer agreed.

"This all sounds good, but once we get Stephen Hill to Sadie's house, how are we going to bring up we know he's the killer?" Sara asked.

Before Eva could answer, Annalise stepped in.

"We come right out and say Sadie and Boscoe told us. We have enough of the details of what happened that he may be so rattled he won't think to dismiss us. That's the hope, anyway."

"Just one more thing," Jennifer added. "If we're all recording this, we'd have to have our phones on the entire time, otherwise we'd have to do it in front of him. Which means the part where we say Sadie and Boscoe told us what happened would also be on the recording."

They all nodded.

"I see where you're going with this," Sarah interrupted. "You're worried about the police hearing that and then dismissing it, right?"

"Right."

"Annalise and I thought about that," Eva said. "That's where we tell another white lie if we have to. We can tell the police we made it up in order to convince Stephen to confess and just got lucky. You could say he's been acting suspiciously, Jennifer, and you took a chance to get him to tell you what happened by telling him the wild story about Sadie and Boscoe and it worked."

She still seemed skeptical, but Jennifer didn't object.

"After Eva and I met, I did a trance session to see if I could find out where Stephen hid the murder weapon," Annalise broke in when no one else added their comments about the recording. "At first I didn't think it was going to work, but then it came to me. It is a crowbar," she said, looking at Eva in confirmation of their earlier conversation. "I saw him cleaning it off and then he stored it in his garage along with his other tools. I don't know if they'll be able to retrieve anything that will tie it into Sadie's murder, but maybe he didn't remove everything. You always see on TV shows where they find DNA in a crack or crevice the killer couldn't reach."

Everyone nodded in agreement.

"How will we get him to come?" Sarah asked after a pause in the conversation.

"I've been thinking about that since Eva suggested it and might have the solution," Jennifer said. "I'll tell him my cousin is planning to sell the property but thought there might be an issue with the plumbing and she'd like to make sure it's fixed and up to code before she lists it with a realtor. As the code enforcement officer for the town, he'd be the one to certify if it was a code violation."

"That's a great idea, but how would you explain why we're there?" Sarah asked.

"I was thinking we'd say one of you is considering making an offer to buy the house. It would make the most sense if that was you, Sarah, since he doesn't know you. I think if you asked him if you needed a license to have a home office it wouldn't set off any alarm bells. Once he's in the house and comfortable with everyone, we would tell him the real reason I asked him to come and hope we can keep him around long enough for him to confess. It's a gamble, but it's going to be tricky no matter what."

"We need to have a plan for who says what and when," Eva suggested.

For the next hour, they brainstormed different scenarios,

testing them out for weaknesses, before settling on a plan of action.

CHAPTER TWENTY-SIX

*E*va was weeding her flower gardens the next day when she heard the whoosh sound of a text notification. Pulling her phone out of her pocket, she saw a group text from Jennifer to all the members of the Cozy Quilts Club.

> We're on for the day after tomorrow at 4:30.
> Let's all meet at my house at 4 to go over the
> plan one last time.

Eva added her thumbs up emoji to the others' replies and put her phone back in her pocket.

Working in her flower gardens was something she'd looked forward to as part of her post-retirement life along with quilting. Picking up her pruning shears and a pail to collect any weeds which might have sprung up since the last time she weeded, she headed to the path that wound its way in a loop around her yard.

It had taken her years to get the plantings to where they now were, expanding each section as she discovered new varieties she wanted to incorporate. A wildflower garden formed the center of the backyard in a shape that conformed to the meandering path around it. On her right, as she stepped out of her back door, was a kitchen garden which included primarily herbs for cooking along with edible flowers she changed out each year depending on her mood and the availability at her local nursery. In the center of the herb garden was a birdbath with a fountain which also served as a water feature. She made a mental note to pick some of the basil later to make pesto. She continued walking to the right, where the path was bordered first by a bed devoted exclusively to peonies and then a cutting garden she used to provide fresh bouquets throughout the summer and early fall. Her mind wasn't completely on the gardens today, though. She found herself coming back again and again to the plan they had hatched to catch Stephen Hill.

At the top of the path, farthest from her house, was the grove of evergreens and birch trees forming the boundary line of the back of her two-acre plot. Not content with having only trees, Eva had created a shade garden of several varieties of ferns and hostas, to which she had added astilbes in the areas of partial shade to provide more color. She had had a small pond dug in that spot when she first moved into the house twenty-five years ago, and the water lilies had spread to cover the surface in shades of yellow and pink. They provided an unintended (by her, at least) haven for frogs that came to the pond to enjoy the water and the lily pads, sunning themselves on top of them and at times appearing to be floating as they held on with their front legs and their back legs hung down in the water. She had placed a concrete bench at one edge of the pond to sit and enjoy the beauty of the gardens, bursting with color when they were in full bloom. Watching the frogs was a bonus which always brought a smile to her face. She often would go there when she had a problem she needed to work out and she found herself gravitating to it today. As she sat on the bench, she went through the details of what was to happen the next day one more time to see if any potential problems came to her which they hadn't thought of when devising their plan. Satisfied they had covered as many holes as possible that they had control over, she continued with her hunt for weeds.

Rounding the path past the pond on her right was another flower bed designed in an English cottage garden style, and she took out her pruning shears to pick flowers for a bouquet and put them in the pail. Walking ten more feet, she reached the end of the path at the vegetable garden located beside the sunroom extension of the house. It irked Eva to no end she had to fence the vegetables as it didn't fit with her garden design aesthetic, but the reality of having them in a semi-rural area meant it was the only way to keep out the deer, rabbits, porcupines, and raccoons if she wanted to harvest any vegetables for herself.

Her thoughts went back once again to Stephen Hill. He was the wild card in the equation, and she chided herself that there was no need to obsess over it; they'd just have to hope for the best. The path wasn't a labyrinth but walking it gave her the same sense of tranquility. Today was no exception and at last the nervousness she felt about executing the plan to trick Stephen Hill to confess faded to the background. She went back into the house with a sense of calm and purpose.

CHAPTER TWENTY-SEVEN

"*I* know we just cleaned up all our scraps, so shouldn't be indulging in more fabric, but I saw the email about the new arrivals at Quilting Essentials and I'd love to check them out. Would you like to join me?" Eva asked Annalise.

"You don't even have to twist my arm," Annalise chuckled. "And it will help take my mind off the trap for Stephen Hill. I'm taking the day off. Would you like to go to lunch after?"

"That sounds great. Jim told me about a new restaurant downtown and since we'd already be in Bangor, it would be close. Would you like me to pick you up so we don't have to find two parking spots?"

"Thanks! That would be terrific. Does ten-thirty work for you? It would give us time to browse at the quilt shop and maybe get to the restaurant before the noon crowd."

"Perfect. I'll see you then."

* * *

"Good morning, ladies. A new shipment of fabrics came in. We have them displayed on the table to your left," the owner of Quilting Essentials, Evelyn Jackson, greeted them.

"That's why we're here. I saw your email announcement," Eva replied.

"Are you working on a particular project or just browsing?"

"Just browsing," Annalise said. "We finished a project, so need more pretty things."

"That works out well for me, too," Evelyn said with a smile.

Paul Taylor walked over to join them. He was the shop's technician who set up and repaired sewing machines and was the instructor for the classes to teach new owners the various features of their machines. His wife, Nicki, also worked at the shop teaching the free motion quilt classes as well as being the on-site long-arm quilter for those who preferred to have someone else do the quilting for their quilt tops. A long-arm machine is a specialized sewing machine attached to a frame which allows the operator to quilt long sections, up to ten feet in some cases, of the quilt without being limited by the small opening regular sewing machines have necessitating bunching up the fabric to fit. Paul was also a quilter, joining the growing ranks of men taking up the craft. He had substituted for Nicki at one of the free motion quilting classes where the members of the Cozy Quilts Club had met. It gave them an opportunity to get to know him better than their occasional meetings when they'd needed their sewing machines serviced.

"Eva, Annalise, good to see you again. What have you been up to?" he asked.

"We had such fun at the free-motion class, we decided to start a quilting club. The four of us have been meeting once a week since then. We're calling it the Cozy Quilts Club," Eva said.

"Really? That's terrific! I like the name."

"You should join us sometime. It would be good to have another perspective," Annalise offered.

"When do you meet?" Paul asked.

"It's on Tuesday nights from six to nine. We do a potluck dinner first and then use the rest of the time to work on projects. The plan is to pick a quilt design or technique to work on each month. It's been held at my house since I've got a dedicated space where we can all work," Eva said.

"You both live in Glen Lake, don't you?" Paul asked.

"Yes," Annalise said.

"You've been having a bit of excitement lately with those murders. It's all customers who live in Glen Lake have been talking about, especially since Evelyn lives there, too. No one seems to have any idea who it could be from what I've heard. Have either of you heard any gossip about who might have done it?"

Eva and Annalise exchanged a brief look, agreeing not to reveal what they knew.

"Nothing official that I've heard," Eva told him.

"I hope they figure it out soon, especially for Jennifer's sake. It was her great-aunt who was murdered, wasn't it? And Howard Smith was one of her neighbors? Not to mention it's unsettling thinking a killer is on the loose," Paul said, as his attention was drawn to the door. "It looks like someone needs my help. I'll talk to you later and I'll give it some thought about coming to one of your meetings," he said, taking his leave and walking to the front of the store where someone had arrived carrying a sewing machine.

Not wanting to say more where they might possibly be over-heard, they turned instead to the display of new batiks which they had come to look at.

"These colors are amazing. I'm sure you've never said this before, but I'm going to buy a yard of this blue and the green. I have no idea what I'll use it for, but I know I'll come up with something later," Eva told Annalise.

"Nope, never said that," Annalise said straight-faced, but then smiled, as they both knew it was not true. "This purple is my favorite, but I'm going to look around the rest of the store in case I see something else I can't live without."

Half an hour later they had made their selections and headed to the counter where Sally Higgins, the store's long-time clerk, assisted with cutting the lengths of fabric and ringing up their purchases.

"Have a nice day, ladies," she said, handing them their reusable shopping bags, which they had remembered to bring with them. Maine had passed a law requiring any bags stores provided would no longer be given out free, the purpose of which was to reduce the amount of plastic going into landfills. It had taken a while to get used to, but Eva kept a ready supply in her car. The habit which had taken longer to develop was bringing them into the store with her.

"I'm looking forward to trying out the new restaurant," Annalise said as she got in the car and buckled her seatbelt.

"Me, too. Fingers crossed it will be good, not too pricey, and we'll find a parking spot nearby."

Annalise held up her crossed fingers in reply.

They got lucky on all three counts.

CHAPTER TWENTY-EIGHT

"Come on in," Jennifer said as she stepped aside to let Eva in. "Annalise and Sarah are in the kitchen."

"I'm sorry I'm late," Eva began.

"Not to worry. Annalise and Sarah haven't been here long." Jennifer led the way into her kitchen and offered Eva a drink before joining them at the table in the breakfast nook.

"I'm too nervous to have anything right now, but thanks," Eva replied. "Those cookies do look delicious, though," she said, looking at the plate in the center of the table piled high with three types of cookies.

"They are!" Sarah said. "I've had one of each of them and not feeling the least bit shameful," she added with a grin.

"I've only had the oatmeal raisin and chocolate chip, but the peanut butter looks too good to pass by," Annalise said, reaching for one.

"I got a little carried away making three different kinds, but in this house, it won't take long before they're all gone."

"Especially at the rate we've been eating them," Sarah agreed.

"I've been trying to decide if we should all be at Sadie's

before Stephen shows up or join me once he's in the house." Jennifer turned the conversation to the matter at hand.

"Me, too," Annalise agreed. "I think, though, it would be better if we were already there. It might be easier to ask him to join us so he doesn't use our arrival as an excuse to leave before we have a chance to put him on the spot."

"That makes sense to me," Sarah put in.

"I think so, too," Eva said.

"Then it's settled. We'll all go over together, and I'll make the introductions and then ask the question about whether adding a dishwasher would cause any problems with the plumbing and Sarah you can ask about the home office angle we discussed at our planning session. While you're doing that, I'll let Boscoe out of Sadie's bedroom, and we'll see how he reacts to Stephen. Eva, you're ready to jump in then with what Boscoe told you about what happened that night?"

"I am. I suspect Stephen isn't going to get a very warm reception, so you might want to make sure he's leashed."

"Good point."

Jennifer's teenaged son and daughter arrived home, distracting her from the conversation. They stopped short when they came into the kitchen and saw the group of ladies at the table, but Jennifer encouraged them to come in.

"This is my quilting club. Let me introduce you to the ladies," she said. "Nicole and Matthew, this is Annalise, Sarah and Eva," she said, gesturing to each in turn. "Ladies, this is my daughter Nicole, who is 16, and my son, Matthew, who just turned 18 and will graduate high school next year."

"Nice to meet you," Nicole and Matthew said in unison.

Eva, Annalise, and Sarah each offered their version of 'Nice to meet you' response.

"Are you planning to go on to college, Matthew?" Eva asked.

"I'm hoping to get into UMaine at the Orono campus but will

apply to two or three other schools, too, to cover the bases. I want to major in Business Administration."

"Good choice. You should be able to go in several directions with that."

"My intuition tells me you'll have no problem with being accepted at any of the schools you apply to," Annalise told him and gave Jennifer a wink.

"Now the real question is whether they'll offer a great scholarship or finance package," Jennifer said with a sigh.

"That won't be a problem either," Annalise said with conviction in her voice.

"There are more cookies in the cookie jar," Jennifer said to the kids, seeing them eyeing the plate of cookies on the table. "Help yourselves, but don't ruin your appetite. I'm going to go to Aunt Sadie's house with the ladies in a few minutes, but dinner will be at six."

"Thanks, Mom," they told her, not needing a second invitation to raid the cookie jar.

"We should probably head over and set things up now anyway," Jennifer told them, and they all rose to follow her. "I'll put Boscoe on his leash, and we'll be set to go."

They left their cars parked in Jennifer's driveway and walked to Sadie's house. Jennifer put Boscoe in Sadie's bedroom and shut the door before joining the others in the large eat-in kitchen. She was about to sit with them at the table when there was a knock at the front door.

CHAPTER TWENTY-NINE

"Okay, ladies, it's showtime. Does everyone have their phone recorders on?" she asked. They all pulled out their phones to check and seeing their nods in affirmation that all systems were go, Jennifer put her phone back in her shorts pocket and headed to the living room. Sarah had hers on the table face-down and Eva and Annalise put theirs in their purses, which they kept on their laps. They had discussed and then discarded the idea of all of them having their phones on the table even if they were upside down. They were concerned it might raise suspicions although it had become ubiquitous to be in social situations with everyone having their cell phones at the ready.

"I'm a little nervous," Sarah whispered.

"Me, too, but it's going to be okay. I've got a good feeling about this," Annalise told her, patting Sarah's hand.

"Thanks for coming, Stephen," they heard Jennifer announce. "I wanted you to check the plumbing to make sure it wouldn't be a problem to add a dishwasher. Sadie's daughter, Melissa, plans to put the house on the market soon and wanted to make sure that wouldn't be a problem for any prospective buyer."

"Oh," Stephen faltered as he saw the group of ladies gathered at the table.

"I'm sorry. I forgot to let you know I'd have anyone else here. You may have seen them earlier when you were checking about all the cars in Sadie's driveway, but we didn't introduce each other. This is Annalise Jordan, Eva Perkins, and Sarah Pascal. Sarah might possibly be interested in buying the house, so it made sense to me to have her here in case she had any questions," Jennifer offered as explanation for their presence.

"Oh, of course," Stephen said, regaining his composure. "Let me take a look under the sink to see what's there," he continued, walking over to the open cabinets under the sink and pulling out a small flashlight from his shirt pocket. "I can't see any reason why there would be a problem installing a dishwasher. The pipes aren't new, but they're up to code."

"So, I also wanted to ask you about the rules about a home business," Sarah piped up when it looked like Stephen was done examining the pipes under the sink. "Do I need any special permits to run a computer security business from my home?"

"Why don't you join us for a glass of lemonade? It's made from scratch," Jennifer offered before he had a chance to respond.

Stephen hesitated a moment, and all four women held their breath, knowing it was crucial for him to drink the offered lemonade so they could take his glass to the police for DNA testing.

"Sure, that sounds delicious," he said and took the empty chair Eva had slid out for him.

Jennifer poured the lemonade, topping off everyone else's glasses as well. Their relief was nearly palpable when they all took a drink and Stephen joined them. Part one of their plan had been achieved.

"To answer your question," Stephen addressed Sarah, "as long as you're occupying the premises, it wouldn't be a problem. You wouldn't even need to make any formal requests. I assume you wouldn't have more than one client at a time coming to see you?"

"That's right. There might be more than one person, but never more than two or three. Maybe four at the most," Sarah answered. "I do most of my meetings by phone or videoconference, so even having one or two people is more an exception than the rule."

"I think I hear Boscoe whining. I put him in Sadie's room, but it sounds like he wants to see who's here," Jennifer interrupted and headed in that direction before waiting for Stephen's reply.

A moment later, Jennifer returned with Boscoe on his leash. Immediately upon seeing Stephen, he lunged toward him, growling, and barking as though intent upon doing him bodily harm. Jennifer had all she could do to control him, so Eva stepped in.

"It's alright, Boscoe. Tell me why you're upset."

Boscoe quieted and turned toward Eva, whimpering, and then letting out short barks, giving every impression he was doing exactly that.

Stephen had not moved out of his seat, but still looked wary as he watched the interaction between Eva and Boscoe.

Boscoe stopped barking and sat beside Jennifer, growling softly in Stephen's direction.

"Boscoe tells me you were here the night Sadie was killed. In fact, he said you're the one who killed her."

Stephen's face blanched, and his jaw dropped, but he said nothing.

"After you hit Sadie on the head and she fell to the floor, Boscoe attacked you and bit you on the arm, but you were able to make him let loose by hitting him on the head, too."

"You can't possibly know that," he stammered. Without

thinking, he put his hand on his arm on the spot where the bite had most likely happened. Realizing his words and action could be interpreted as a confession, he quickly dropped it back into his lap. "There's no way you can prove it. There were no witnesses."

"Boscoe was a witness."

"Even if that ridiculous idea was true, and I'm not saying it is, who in their right mind would believe a dog told you I murdered Sadie?" he asked with a self-assured expression on his face.

Jennifer felt a tingling on the finger where she had put the ring her cousin had given her after Sadie's death, letting her know Sadie had wanted her to have it.

"It was Sadie's bedtime, but she answered the door because she saw it was you. She had closed the door after letting you in and turned around to see you coming toward her. You were wearing a light blue short-sleeved shirt, and you had something in your hand. She didn't even have time to protect herself before you struck her. She wants to know why you would do that? You'd never had any quarrels in the past. She doesn't understand what she did to provoke you into harming her," Jennifer said, looking at Stephen.

Again, his face blanched.

"I didn't intend to kill her. It all happened so fast. I wasn't thinking straight. I'd gone to give Howard Smith a citation. We were on his front porch, and he began arguing with me. I tried to calm him down, but then he came at me with a crowbar. We struggled and I'm still not sure how it happened, but I was able to get it away from him. I slipped and when I was trying to regain my balance, I must have hit him accidentally on the head. He fell, and when I checked on him, he was dead. That's when I heard Boscoe barking and I could see him outside looking in my direction. The flood light was on, and I saw Sadie standing in her doorway. I panicked. I convinced myself I had to kill her, too, so there wouldn't be any witnesses." He looked at Jennifer, his eyes pleading. "You've got to believe me when I tell you I wasn't in my right mind. All I could think of was that my reputation would be ruined, and I had no witnesses to back me up it was self-defense. I thought I could make it look like it was an addict breaking in for drugs. There's been a lot of that happening lately."

No one spoke, but something shifted in Stephen's demeanor and his face hardened, challenging them to do anything about his confession.

"You can try to convince the cops I did it, but like I said before, who would believe you? If any of you try to have me arrested, I'll deny everything. Do you really think you can go into a police station and tell them a dog told you I killed Sadie? They'd laugh you out the door," he directed his comment at Eva. "I think I'm done here. Good luck with selling the house, Jennifer." He got up and stormed out the door.

They all sat in stunned silence. Sarah brought them back to the moment by picking up her phone and stopping the recording, and the others followed suit.

"We should probably check to make sure we got all that," Annalise suggested.

The conversation had been captured on all their phones. Jennifer retrieved a plastic zip-lock bag from one of the drawers. Taking a napkin from the napkin holder in the center of the table, she used it to pick up Stephen's empty glass and carefully placed the glass inside the bag and sealed it.

"Now what?" Sarah asked.

"I'll talk to Jim and ask if he thinks we should all take the evidence to the police. I want him to hear at least my recording of Stephen's confession first. If he thinks we should all go, I'll send a group text and we can go from there."

"And if he agrees with Stephen that they would think we're crazy, even with his confession?" Annalise asked.

"We'll cross that bridge when we come to it," Eva said.

"We should probably lock up and go back to my house before Stephen thinks about coming back here. I don't think he'd dare come to my house with David at home."

Nodding in agreement, they gathered up their glasses, washing and returning them to the cabinet first and then returned to Jennifer's house. Saying their goodbyes, they each returned to their respective homes.

CHAPTER THIRTY

"Good morning, Jennifer. This is a surprise."

"Good morning, Eva. I was wondering if you would meet me for lunch. I'd like to talk to you about yesterday."

"Of course. Are you having concerns about it?"

"Well, yes. I'm having second thoughts but wanted to discuss it with you before changing my mind. Can you meet me at The Checkout Diner at eleven-thirty?"

"Yes, that works for me. I'll see you then."

"I hope she's not going to back out about going to the police," Eva said aloud, but more for her own benefit, since Reuben was the only one with her.

Even if she does, couldn't someone else do it? You all have the recording on your phone.

"That's true. I'll see what Jennifer has to say first and then I can talk it over with Jim. It could be considered withholding evidence if we don't go to the police, so if she is getting cold feet, one of us should still report Stephen Hill to the authorities."

It makes sense to find out what she's worried about first and then you can figure out what to do next.

"Good advice, Reuben. You always know what to do."

Obviously!

"And your modesty shines through, as always."

Harrumph. Done with dispensing his words of wisdom, Reuben turned his back to Eva and settled in on his cushion.

* * *

Jennifer had already been seated when Eva arrived at the diner.

"Jennifer is at the table in the corner," Betty nodded her head in that direction when Eva walked in. "She let me know you were coming to meet her."

"Thanks, Betty."

Eva saw Jennifer sitting at the table facing the diner's entrance with a worried look on her face as she waved at Eva.

"Thank you for coming," Jennifer said. "I'm not sure I slept a wink last night."

"Oh, no. Tell me what has you worried?"

"I felt so confident about going to the police with his confession when we were all together, but once I got home and started thinking about actually doing it, I panicked. I haven't told David what we did either, because I wasn't sure how he'd react. Are you sure this is the right thing to do?"

"I do, but I can understand your hesitation. This is an enormous leap of faith that the police will even listen, let alone believe you. I'm sure Jim would go with you, though, so you wouldn't be alone."

"That's true. Having him with me would be a big help. And you said he knows the detectives working on the case?"

"He does. They're not best friends or anything, but they know each other as work associates, and they trust his opinion. At least that's the impression I got when we talked earlier about the case."

"That should help," Jennifer agreed, but Eva could tell she wasn't convinced.

"It's probably best that you be the one to do this, since it makes the most sense for you to approach the detectives investigating the murder. You're the one who is closely invested in having the murder solved and you've already talked to them, but would you rather have one of the rest of us go instead?"

Jennifer thought for a moment and then shook her head.

"No, it should be me."

"It goes without saying it will be hard, but the police aren't making any progress. This may be the only way Sadie's murderer will be brought to justice."

"You're right. I have to do this for Sadie. It's true, it will be uncomfortable but I'll get over it," Jennifer said with a resolved nod of her head, as though to affirm to herself it was the right thing to do.

Eva reached out to put her hand on Jennifer's.

"You know all of us are backing you up on this and if you need someone to go with you along with Jim, you can count on us. We want justice for Sadie... and Howard Smith, too," she said as an afterthought. "He might not have been the most pleasant man to be around from what I've heard, but *someone* should be held accountable and let a jury decide the outcome," Eva said.

Although the only other occupants were at the other end of the diner and their conversation was unlikely to be heard over the country music playing in the background, Jennifer knew Eva had purposely not mentioned Stephen Hill's name to be on the safe side. Just then, Betty appeared at their table with glasses of water for each of them.

"I wanted to tell you how sorry I was to hear about Sadie. I didn't get the chance when you first came in. How are you holding up?"

"It was a shock at first and I still feel a little numb, but it's getting easier."

"Have the police come up with any new leads?"

"Not that they've shared with me," Jennifer replied.

"Well, you keep the faith. I'm sure they'll find the killer sooner or later," Betty said, giving Jennifer a pat on the shoulder. "Now, what can I get you ladies to eat?"

They gave Betty their orders and waited until she left before speaking.

"It will be alright, whatever you decide," Eva was reassuring Jennifer but stopped talking when she saw Jennifer staring toward the diner's entrance and her face had blanched.

CHAPTER THIRTY-ONE

"*W*hat's wrong?" Eva asked, her voice concerned.

Jennifer looked down at her hands folded on the table and whispered, "Don't turn around, but Stephen Hill walked in. I think he saw me."

As if on cue, he walked to their table.

"Do you mind if I join you? I wanted to tell you how sorry I am about Sadie," he said, his voice louder than necessary, as though he wanted to make sure Jennifer would have to answer affirmatively if anyone was watching.

"Of course, and thank you, but you've already given me your condolences," Jennifer said, feeling cornered.

Eva remained silent but was on alert. Stephen sat at the empty chair beside Eva so he was facing Jennifer and preventing any observers from seeing his face.

"I can't believe you tricked me into coming to that set up yesterday," he said, his voice low and angry. His hands were clenched on the table, and he leaned forward threateningly toward Jennifer. "You have the audacity to try to ruin my reputation. Do you really think anyone will believe you?" he spat. "And what's the point? It's not going to bring her back, and it's not as though I'm going to go on a killing rampage. It was an *accident*. I told you that."

"Do you really think you're going to get away with this, Stephen?" Jennifer replied, her voice low as well.

"I do and I will."

"How can you live with yourself knowing what you did to Sadie?" She leaned toward Stephen and placed her hands on the table as well, although hers were folded, not clenched. "I can see how what happened with Howard could have been self-defense, but what did killing Sadie accomplish? She was a sweet, gentle old woman who was no threat to you. She probably didn't even see anything. You know her eyesight was poor, and chances are she only saw two people on Howard's porch. I doubt she would have been able to identify you."

"I told you. I panicked. I wasn't in my right mind and couldn't risk the chance she'd seen me."

"Yes, that's what you said, but I'm not sure I believe you," she said, her eyes taking on a hard edge.

"You can believe whatever you like, but you and I both know if you go to the police, they'll send you packing. Think about it, Jennifer. Do you seriously want to risk *your* reputation or David's? This is a small town, and you know how people gossip. You'll be the laughingstock of the town if you say one of your friends talked to Sadie's ghost or that Sadie's *dog* told your friend I did it." He looked at Eva with condescension before turning back to Jennifer. "It could ruin your business. I'll make sure of it," he said, his voice menacing. His hands unclenched and he leaned back in his chair, confident his threats would convince her to stay silent.

Before Jennifer was able to reply, Betty appeared at their table with Eva and Jennifer's lunch order and Jennifer leaned back in her seat to give Betty room to put down her meal.

"Are you going to be joining them?" she asked Stephen. "I can set another place for you."

"No, I just wanted to tell Jennifer again how sorry I am about Sadie. I'll sit over at one of the booths," Stephen said, smiling at Betty as he rose to his feet and pushed his chair back toward the table. He then turned to Jennifer. "Think about what I said and if I can be of help, be sure to let me know."

"Are you ladies all set?" Betty asked after Stephen had walked away toward one of the booths.

"I'm good," Eva said.

"Me, too."

Betty took out her order pad and placed their check on the table.

"I'll take this when you're ready but there's no hurry," she said.

Jennifer waited until Betty left to attend to the couple who had walked in and then looked at Eva, a determined expression on her face.

"I've made up my mind. Ask Jim if he'll go with me to the police. If that scumbag thinks he can threaten me to keep me from telling them what I know and I'll just roll over, he's sadly mistaken. Sadie deserves justice and I'm going to do everything I can so she has it."

"You're sure?"

"I'm sure. I'll need to tell David first, and that's going to be an interesting discussion," she said, a wry expression on her face, "but it has to be done."

"Okay. I'll talk to Jim."

Jennifer looked toward the booth where Stephen had sat facing them and saw him returning her glance. Her eyes narrowed and turned hard, and she did not back down. His expression was not as confident as when he'd left their table, and he was the first to look away.

They finished their meal, turning their discussion to other topics. Jennifer was aware that Stephen was casting glances their way, but she purposely avoided looking directly at him. They were the first to leave and as they walked out of the diner after paying for their meal, Jennifer gave Stephen one last look, her face set with determination, and no longer having any doubts she'd made the right decision. She no longer saw him as a threat, but instead a pathetic, frightened man whose attempt at intimidation had failed.

CHAPTER THIRTY-TWO

*L*ater that afternoon, Eva was about to call Jim when the phone rang in her hand, and she saw Annalise's name displayed on the screen.

"Hello, Annalise."

"Have you already talked to Jim? I think I may have something important to share and was hoping to catch you."

"I was about to call him when your call came in."

She must be psychic, Reuben opined.

Eva shot him a look before returning her attention to Annalise.

"Last night I had a vision of Stephen with the crowbar. He was using a rag soaked with bleach to clean the blood off and then put it in his garage with his other tools so it would blend in. It's in a plastic tote on a metal shelving unit beside the workbench. Depending on how well he cleaned it off or if any blood seeped into a crack out of reach of the rag, it could tie him to the murders."

"That's great! Hopefully, his DNA from the glass will be a match and the police can get a search warrant. Knowing where to start the search will be a big help."

"Let's hope he doesn't move it or get rid of it altogether now that he knows we're onto him."

"Fingers crossed," Eva said. "You're not going to believe what happened earlier. Jennifer asked me to come to lunch because she was having second thoughts about going to the police. She was worried about their reaction. It had all made sense yesterday when we were together, but after she had time to think about it, she wasn't as sure."

"That's not too surprising. Were you able to convince her she had to do it?"

"I'm not sure it was me or Stephen Hill who accomplished that."

"Stephen Hill?"

"Yes. He came in when we were waiting for our lunch. He walked right over to our table and sat down. Then he basically threatened Jennifer he would destroy her reputation and David's if she said anything. He implied he'd make sure everyone would think she was crazy if she mentioned how she knew he was the killer. And that it could destroy David's business, too."

"What a piece of work! So he thinks he's going to get away with it?"

"That's the impression I got when he left our table. Instead, it made Jennifer even more determined. She's not on the fence anymore."

"Good!"

"I should probably call Jim now so we can start this process as soon as possible."

"Right. Let me know how it goes."

"Will do," Eva assured her, and they disconnected the call.

"Good afternoon, sunshine," Jim greeted Eva when he answered her call.

"You sound like you're in a good mood today," Eva replied.

"Had a good poker night last night. A few extra bucks in my pocket always puts me in a good mood."

"Well, hopefully, what I have to share with you won't ruin that. Can you come over to see me?"

"That sounds ominous. Should I be worried?"

"Not about us, if that's what you mean. It's too complicated to explain over the phone and I'd rather do it in person."

"Okay. I should be able to be there within half an hour," Jim told her.

"See you then."

CHAPTER THIRTY-THREE

"*Y*ou did WHAT?!" Jim exclaimed after Eva told him about the confrontation with Stephen Hill. "You could have all been killed! He's apparently done it twice already and might try again to cover his tracks."

Reuben had been sitting on Jim's lap but decamped to his spot in the bay window, not wanting to be in the line of fire, verbal or otherwise.

You've got some splainin to do, he directed at Eva as he passed by, only to be met with a glare. Realizing he may have touched a nerve, he picked up his pace and jumped up onto the safety of his cushion.

"I don't think so," Eva answered Jim with conviction. "He killed Sadie when he was in a state of panic, but he is convinced no one would believe us and he didn't know we were recording the conversation, so we have his confession. So, would you go to the detectives in charge and tell them Stephen confessed and you have his DNA?"

"So that's why you were asking about the law with respect to recording a conversation without someone's knowledge." It was a statement rather than a question.

"Yes. We knew we'd have to have a reason for the police to bother testing the glass for DNA, and that's what we came up with."

"You know he's right. The cops are going to think twice about his confessing after being told the dog identified him as the killer."

"We thought about that and agreed to claim we made that part up to trick him into confessing. You can say Jennifer told you she had gotten suspicious because Stephen had been acting out of character lately and seemed uncomfortable whenever Sadie was mentioned and had been asking a lot of questions about whether the police had talked to her with updates about the murder. So will you go? You didn't answer me before."

Jim was quiet for a few minutes, considering that strategy, and then nodded. "It might work. I know the Sheriff's office has come up short with their investigation and they haven't had any leads to follow up on. This would at least give them something new to investigate. You said you have the confession recorded on your phone?"

"We all have a recording of it, just in case. I can play it now if you like."

"Yeah, let me listen. I want to know exactly what they'd be getting before agreeing to pass it on."

Eva picked up her phone from the coffee table, navigated to the voice memos, and played the recording for him. "What do you think?" she asked when it had ended.

"I'm not convinced they'd be able to get a search warrant based on that alone, but if the DNA comes back with a match to the blood spots found at Sadie's house, it should be enough to satisfy a judge it's warranted. Do you have the glass?"

"Yes. We were going to leave it at Jennifer's, but decided it might be better for one of us to take it instead, to be on the safe side."

"Good thinking."

"Sounds like maybe you've changed your mind and don't think our plan was harebrained after all."

"Oh, no, I still think it was harebrained and potentially dangerous, but you've got something to show for it that might just wrap this case up."

"I almost forgot one other thing. Annalise called me this afternoon to let me know she had a vision about Stephen and the crowbar. In her vision, she saw him cleaning it with a rag soaked in bleach. He then put it in a plastic tote that's on a shelving unit in his garage next to his workbench, mixed in with other tools, so it looks like it belongs there."

Jim rolled his eyes. "And just how am I supposed to explain that to the investigators?"

"You probably can't," Eva agreed. "But maybe you could make a suggestion he might have done it, just as a hypothesis."

"I'll take that under advisement," he said, and Eva could tell he was doing just that.

"I'm beginning to feel like Colombo, but I have one more thing to tell you. Jennifer and I were having lunch at The Checkout Diner today and Stephen Hill came in. He came over to our table and basically threatened Jennifer he would make sure everyone in town knew we claimed to have communicated with ghosts and dogs to get him to talk if she went to the police."

"What did Jennifer do?"

"Nothing. Betty came to the table with our orders, so Stephen left and went to a booth to have his lunch. Jennifer had been on the fence about going to the police. That's why we met for lunch. But his threats and the idea he might get away with Sadie's murder otherwise put her over the edge and she's more ready than ever now. So, again, would you be willing to set up an appointment with the guys who are doing the investigation?"

"Before I answer, I want you to promise you'll stay away from Stephen Hill. He could be dangerous, especially if he thinks he's at risk of getting caught. That said, I think Jennifer should go with me to explain the connection and why she was suspicious enough to stage this intervention as well as take the glass with Hill's DNA."

"That's what we thought, too. Should I give her a call now so the two of you can coordinate when to go?"

"Probably best to do it sooner than later, before I have enough time to rethink this and talk myself out of it. I have to admit I'm a little worried about Stephen Hill being right and they'll think I'm a nutcase, too."

"But you're not the one claiming a dog gave you the inside scoop that got him to confess," Eva objected.

"No, but I'm the nutcase who believed it enough to go along with the plan after the fact."

Eva smiled and gave Jim a kiss on his cheek. "And I love you for it."

"Don't go trying to butter me up with sweet talk," Jim groused, but Eva knew he was just giving her a hard time.

Oh, brother, what a sucker Reuben muttered, still perched on his cushion observing their exchanges.

Eva turned to face him and gave him a satisfied smile.

* * *

"I HAVE YOU ON SPEAKER. Jim's with us," Eva announced when Jennifer answered her call. "He said he'll get in touch with the detectives and make an appointment for the two of you to take the glass and recording to them."

"Thank you... and him... for doing this. I don't think I would have had the nerve to go on my own."

"You should be prepared to tell them you had suspicions about Stephen because he had been asking questions about the investigation and was acting out of character lately, which is why we hatched this plan."

"Just like we'd discussed?" Jennifer asked.

"Yes. That's what I told Jim when he asked and you can claim you had no idea I was going to say the dog told me to shock the confession out of him," Eva said, chuckling. "That's if they ask, of course."

"I'm hoping they'll gloss over that and go right into the confession part," Jennifer said.

"Me, too. I'm going to hand my phone over to Jim and the two of you can exchange contact info so he can call you back when he's had a chance to talk to the detectives to set up the meeting."

"Thanks again, Eva. I hope this works so Stephen will be behind bars soon and Sadie will have justice for her murder. She really did come through to me when I touched her ring. I wasn't making that up for Stephen's benefit. If nothing else, she knows now why he did it but that's not much consolation. She's still dead."

"I know, but maybe now she can rest in peace."

"Amen to that."

CHAPTER THIRTY-FOUR

*T*he next day, Jim and Jennifer met at Eva's house before going to the police station with the recording of Stephen's confession and the glass with his DNA. Jim had given the detectives working the case only the barest of information, telling them he had someone who might have new evidence about a possible suspect for Sadie and Howard's murders.

"I'm really nervous," Jennifer told Jim.

"It's okay. I'll be with you," he reassured her.

"Just remember what we'd come up with to explain how we got Stephen to confess. The important piece is his confession on the recording and once they get the DNA reports back and his matches the blood found at Sadie's house, they should have enough evidence to build a case," Eva said.

"Right," Jennifer said with more confidence in her voice and looking less worried.

"If you're all set, we should probably leave now," Jim said.

Jennifer gathered up her purse and gave Eva a quick peck on the cheek.

"Thank you for all you've done. It means a lot."

"You're most welcome. Good luck! Give me a call when you're done."

Jim gave Eva a kiss on the cheek as well and whispered in her ear, "We're going to need that luck."

Eva gave his hand a squeeze in silent acknowledgement and watched them walk to Jim's car, waving as Jim backed the car out of her driveway.

"Do you think this will work?" Jennifer asked once they were on their way.

"I'm cautiously optimistic," he replied with a grin.

"Do you know the detectives we'll be seeing?"

"Not well, but I worked with them enough to know they'll try to have an open mind."

"I guess that's all I can ask."

The ride to the Sheriff's department only took fifteen minutes, most of which passed in silence, each lost in their own thoughts.

"We're here to see Detectives Smith and Roberts. We have an appointment for two pm," Jim told the clerk in the reception area.

After checking the schedule, the clerk gave a nod. "If you'll have a seat, I'll let them know you're here. They should be right out. Please put these on," she said as she handed over two visitor passes on lanyards for Jim and Jennifer to put around their necks.

They only had to wait a couple minutes before they were met by a tall, dark-haired man wearing a suit.

"Hello, Jim," he said as he held out his hand to shake.

"Hello, Phil. Let me introduce you to Jennifer Ryder. Sadie Emerson was her great aunt."

Phil Roberts turned to Jennifer and extended his hand. "Yes, we met earlier when Dennis and I interviewed her after she'd found Mrs. Emerson's body. Again, I'm sorry for your loss."

"Thank you," she said, shaking his proffered hand.

"Let's go this way. Dennis is waiting for us in the conference room," he said, turning to lead them through the door to the offices behind the reception area.

They exchanged greetings with Dennis Smith and sat at the conference table with Jennifer and Jim facing the detectives.

At least they didn't put us in an interrogation room Jennifer thought as she looked around the room surprised to see it was decorated much like any business's conference room.

"Jim said you might have new information about a possible suspect," Dennis opened the conversation.

Jennifer retrieved her phone from her purse along with the sealed plastic bag containing the glass with Stephen Hill's DNA and placed them on the table.

"What's this?" Phil Roberts asked, looking from Jennifer to Jim.

"The phone has a recording of the killer's confession, and the glass has his DNA," Jennifer told him.

Phil Roberts's eyebrows raised, but he didn't say anything at first. "You have the killer's confession? Who is it and may I ask how you got that?"

"The killer is Stephen Hill. He's also my neighbor and Sadie's and I had suspicions about his behavior recently. He'd been acting out of character and inserting himself as though he was worried we might know something about Sadie's murder. My friends and I pretended we needed his advice about Sadie's plumbing in case there was an issue before we put the house on the market and another of my friends pretended she was interested in buying it but needed to know if she could have a home business on site," she explained, her nervousness causing her to ramble but the detectives remained silent so she would continue. "I realize the next part is going to sound crazy, but we convinced him we had knowledge he was with Sadie the night she was murdered and that she and Boscoe... that's her dog... told me he was the one who did it."

Both of the detectives' eyebrows raised at that.

"Your deceased aunt's dog?" Dennis Smith asked, as though not sure he'd heard correctly.

"Like I said, it sounds crazy. We knew Stephen wouldn't confess on his own, so we had to do something to shock him into believing we had information no one else would know." Jennifer said. "Here, let me play the recording for you. I think that will explain it better." She picked up her phone and navigated to the recording and hit the play icon. When it got to the part where Stephen Hill confessed he'd killed both Howard Smith and Sadie Emerson, the detectives looked at each other, the question of whether the other believed what they were hearing passing unspoken between them.

"I used a napkin to pick up the glass he had used to drink the lemonade and put it right into the plastic bag. I used a napkin when I gave it to him, too, to make sure only his prints would be on it, but I thought the DNA would be the more important part. Just in case you found any blood from where Boscoe bit him," she added quickly, remembering that they weren't supposed to know about the blood spatter.

"That's all very interesting," Phil Roberts said after a moment. "We would usually ask you to leave your phone with us as evidence, but can you make a copy for us?"

"I can email it to you, I think," Jennifer said, checking her phone to find the options available. "Oh, yes, here it is. I can share the recording that way. We can try it before I leave to make sure it works," she suggested.

Phil gave her his email address and Jennifer sent the file. After a few seconds, his email notification sounded, and he was able to confirm the file had been received.

"We'd like to make sure you don't delete that file in case we need it for evidence at trial," he told her.

"Oh, no, of course. I understand completely. My other friends have recordings on their phones as well. We wanted to make sure at least one of us got his confession."

"Thank you very much, Mrs. Ryder. It's probably in our earlier notes, but if you would give us your contact information in case we have any other questions," he said as he slid a pad of paper and a pen over to her.

Jennifer wrote her name and telephone number, as well as her address, on the paper and slid it back.

"What happens now?" she asked.

"We'll send the glass to our lab to check on the DNA first and if we find a match verifying you were correct about the blood splatter which must have been from when Boscoe bit Mr. Hill, we'll have enough evidence to continue the investigation. I think we would want to have that in hand as well before we question him with the confession."

"I understand. You don't think he might try to make a run for it before then, do you?"

"I don't," Phil Roberts replied. "I think he has probably convinced himself you wouldn't have told us about his confession. He didn't know you were recording him?"

"No. We all had our phones hidden so he couldn't see the screens to know we had them recording him. And he had no idea I was going to take the glass for his DNA," she added.

"That was good thinking," Dennis said.

"Well, I think that's all we need for now," Phil said, rising to his feet, cueing Jennifer and Jim the meeting was over, and then escorting them to the lobby.

"Do you think they believed me?" Jennifer asked once they were back in the car.

"I think they're at least giving you the benefit of the doubt," Jim replied. "I'll be honest with you now. I wasn't expecting they would."

"Let's hope they're able to get his DNA and match it to the blood so they can arrest him."

"I think that would be the perfect outcome," Jim agreed.

* * *

"How did it go?" Eva asked when Jim and Jennifer returned.

"I think it went okay," Jennifer told her.

Jim nodded in agreement. "Now it's just a waiting game, but at least they have something to work with. They'd reached the end of the road in the investigation before this. I think it will get them back on track and ready to home in on Stephen Hill now that they actually have someone to focus their investigation on."

"That's all we can ask for, I guess. Fingers crossed. For now, though, I better go home. I'll see you at the next Cozy Quilts Club meeting," Jennifer said as she got into her car and left.

"Now that she's gone and you can be honest, what's your take on whether it worked?"

"I meant what I said. I really think they're taking it seriously and will investigate it," Jim reassured her.

"Good! Stephen Hill needs to be held accountable. It may have been self-defense with Howard Smith, but what he did to Sadie is inexcusable."

"I agree and hopefully, that's what will happen."

CHAPTER THIRTY-FIVE

"*W*ould you like to come to my house for a visit? I need a distraction from this waiting game for the DNA results to come in," Annalise asked Eva.

"I'd love that. I've never been to your house."

Eva calculated in her head how long it would take for the drive. "I could be there in ten to fifteen minutes. Is that too soon?"

"Not at all. I'll see you when you get here."

"I'm going to be out for a while," she told Reuben. "Annalise has invited me for a visit."

I'll be here, waiting with bells on he said, using his snarky tone.

Eva remained unphased, used to Reuben's moods by now. Tossing her phone in her purse, she gave him a wave and headed out the door.

As she drove, Eva reflected on how much she was enjoying Annalise's company. They had an instant connection when they first met at the quilting class, which she'd attributed to their being closer in age, but seeing more of her since then had made her realize it was more than that. It felt like they were kindred souls. Within the ten minutes she'd estimated, she arrived at Annalise's home, a two-story white farmhouse with a wrap-around porch on two sides. Although well-maintained, it was obvious it was old. Eva estimated it had probably been built in the 1800s. The front door centered in the building, with a window on either side, was all Annalise. It had been painted a shade of purple, and the shutters matched. She had only had time to step out of the car and close her door when Annalise walked out onto the porch to greet her.

"What a beautiful house!" Eva told her. "That color on the doors and shutters is all you."

"Thank you and yes, it wasn't original to the house. I had to put my own stamp on it."

"How long have you lived here?"

"I've been living here for a little over a year, but it's the house I grew up in. It's been in my family since it was built. I moved back after my mother passed away. I made some changes when I moved in to update it, but it's mostly the same layout. The barn had to be torn down about ten years ago, so I had the garage built when I took over. Come on in. I'll give you the tour."

"The newel post on the staircase is gorgeous!" Eva said, admiring the craftmanship of the carved design. "I've never seen the fluting spiral like that. I've only seen straight vertical lines."

"My great-great-grandfather was a farmer by trade, but he liked to do woodworking, so he made that himself. He made the mantels for the fireplaces, too."

"What a talent he had. I'm surprised he didn't do it for a living. There must have been a call for it. I'm guessing the house was built in the early 1800s and workmanship like this was valued then."

"He probably would have liked to, but it was expected he

would be a farmer and it provided a living for the family. He did his woodworking more as a hobby in the limited spare time he had. They had animals, so when they weren't farming in the winter, there were still plenty of chores to keep him busy. Even if they had a woodstove, which I don't remember from my childhood, I can't imagine it would have been very comfortable working in the barn in the winter."

Eva followed Annalise as she walked to the right.

"This used to be the formal parlor, but now it's where I do my Reiki sessions. I close the pocket doors during a session to provide additional privacy even though I never have more than one person at a time. It's important for them to be comfortable."

Eva walked into the room, which had a massage table set up in the center, two comfortable chairs with a side table between them and a long, narrow table under the window which faced the street.

"It feels so cozy. I can't put my finger on why, but it has an aura of calm and serenity."

"Thank you. That's exactly what I'm trying to achieve. It's important to make my clients feel relaxed."

"What exactly is Reiki? I have to confess I don't know anything about it."

Annalise considered for a moment before answering. "Well, in its simplest terms, Reiki practitioners are facilitators who channel energy through their hands into the patient's body to activate their natural healing processes, both emotionally and physically. The client remains dressed and usually there is no direct touch, although that can be done with the patient's permission if it's called for. I'd love to do a session for you sometime. The first one's free," she said, with a smile and a wink.

"I think I'd like that. I'm not sure I understand how it would work, but I'm willing to give it a try. Would I have to have something specific for you to work on?"

"Not at all. It's not unusual even when someone does come

in for a treatment for one reason, they will experience an emotional or physical release they weren't expecting."

"Well, I'm intrigued. Do you have your booking calendar handy? Let's set something up now or I'll put it off."

"Sure, it's right here," Annalise said, walking over to the table and pulling out a planner from the drawer.

Once that was settled, they continued the tour. Across the hall from the Reiki studio and to the left of the entry was the living room, which Annalise had decorated in her eclectic style. The furniture included a cushy couch with brightly colored pillows from one end to the other, a chair on either side also with extra pillows, a painted coffee table and hutch which held the television and video and audio equipment. The artwork on the walls continued the theme of splashes of color and a mix of design aesthetics.

"I love this. I'm guessing this amount of color wasn't how it looked when you grew up."

Annalise chuckled. "That would be an understatement, but this suits me much more than my mother's style of decorating."

Eva followed her into the kitchen, separated from the living room by the half bath.

"This is where I did the most updating on this floor. It had been remodeled in the 70s, but I did a complete gut. It cost an arm and a leg, but it was worth it."

Across from the kitchen was the formal dining room.

"I hardly ever use this, but it's here when I do have a large group."

"I know what you mean. A formal dining room seems like such a waste of space, but it can come in handy at times."

They walked down a short hallway that led back to the entry and the staircase leading to the bedrooms. At the top of the staircase was the guest bathroom and two guest bedrooms on the right. To the left was Annalise's room.

"The original layout had four bedrooms, but I took one to

add an en suite bath and sitting room as well as a decent closet. Old houses never had much closet room. They didn't have as many clothes then so didn't need them. I, on the other hand, have no problem owning enough clothes that I needed a walk-in closet."

"It is perfect. I'm so jealous of all the space you have and that view!" Eva exclaimed as they walked into the sitting room space. It overlooked the back side of the property and could have been taken from a painting of a pastoral scene, exuding the same sense of serenity she had felt in the Reiki studio.

"I spend a lot of time here. Each season has its own special beauty, even mud season!" she said before Eva had a chance to ask.

The tour complete, they returned to the living room to continue their visit.

"I've been so busy admiring your house I almost forgot to tell you about my conversation with Jim. He called last night to give me an update about Stephen Hill."

"Have they arrested him?"

"Not yet, but the detectives on the case interviewed him again after Jim and Jennifer met with them. They didn't mention that, of course. They told him it was a follow up to see if he might have remembered anything else and to verify his alibi for that night."

"Did they learn anything new?"

"Not as far as information they didn't already have, but he apparently was acting nervous and might have slipped up about his alibi. He'd originally told them he had gone to Howard Smith's house around eight-thirty and left to go to the convenience store when no one answered the door. When they pressed him about why he would have bothered at that time of night to be giving out citations and why not do it in the daytime during normal business hours…"

"I wondered about that, too," Annalise interrupted.

"He said he'd been trying to do that but hadn't ever found Howard Smith at home the other times he'd tried. That night, he had to go to the store anyway, and it looked like Howard might be home, so he wanted to give it one more try. They questioned him about why he thought Howard was home, since he had already said no one answered the door. That seemed to rattle him, but he stuck to his story that the light in the kitchen was on, but no one answered, so he just left the citation in the door and went on his way."

"It's not enough to implicate him so they can make an arrest, though."

"No, but the fact he was acting nervously made them more willing to accept the confession he'd made on Jennifer's phone. I'm not sure why that would make a difference since it was obviously his voice on the recording, but it was something they could add to their report, so it was on the record. I think they're still worried about this all amounting to nothing if the DNA test doesn't match the blood they found at Sadie's."

"That really is the critical piece, but now that they do know he confessed, maybe they would lean on him even more, hoping he will slip up."

"Let's hope they don't have to go that route. Stephen is determined not to confess, and he has a lot to lose. He knows he messed up when he confessed to us, so my guess is he'll be more cautious with the police although he doesn't know we taped him and they have that recording. I'm skeptical they would take the confession to the district attorney's office if they weren't one hundred percent sure it would result in an arrest warrant. Without any physical evidence to tie him to the crime, they'd have a hard time proving anything, and I have my doubts about the prosecutor being willing to admit the confession he made on the phone as evidence in a trial."

Annalise nodded her agreement. Not having anything more to add, they moved on to other topics.

"This has been so much fun, but I should probably leave," Eva said two hours later, after checking her watch. "Thank you for inviting me."

"It was my pleasure and I'm looking forward to our Reiki session."

"Me, too."

CHAPTER THIRTY-SIX

*E*va opened her door to the sound of her phone ringing.

"They got him!" Jim announced as soon as Eva answered the phone.

"When?"

"I just got the call from Phil Roberts letting me know they were able to get the search warrant based on the DNA match to the blood droplets. They didn't have to use the confession you'd taped and between you and me, I think they were relieved. They found the crowbar right where Annalise said it would be, and it had blood residue so they will send it to the crime lab for analysis. If it matches either Howard Smith or Sadie, that should be a slam dunk, but they were still able to arrest him and take him into custody."

"Have they let Jennifer know?" Eva asked.

"Yes, Phil had called her first and then called me."

"Oh, I'm so happy to hear this."

"It's not over yet. This is step one. He'll be hiring a lawyer and then it will go to trial where it will be up to a jury to decide his fate, but it may never have gotten this far if it wasn't for your club getting involved."

"So, tell me how it all went down," Eva asked conspiratorially.

Sounds like you've been watching too many crime shows on TV, Reuben interjected from his spot in the bay window.

Eva held her hand over the phone's receiver before responding, "No comments from the peanut gallery."

"Sorry, I didn't quite catch that. Your voice was muffled," Jim said.

"I was talking to Reuben. He was giving me a hard time."

"Even though I saw it with my own eyes, it's still hard to believe you can talk to your cat," Jim said before going on to tell Eva about Stephen Hill's arrest. "Like I said, the DNA was a match, so a judge approved a search warrant. Phil, Dennis, the crime scene investigation team, and back up officers went to Stephen's house this morning and caught him before he left for work. At first, he was trying to block them from entering, saying they had no right to be there and had the wrong person. He backed down once they showed him the search warrant. I think he still believed he was going to get away with it until they went right into his garage to the box of tools where he'd hidden the crowbar. They already had him in handcuffs and had read him his rights before they told him about the DNA match to the blood found at the scene. He didn't believe they could have his DNA but then they told him about the glass he'd used at Sadie's and that Jennifer had recorded his confession. Once he heard that, he realized there was no point arguing and decided to take advantage of staying silent until he had an attorney. They took him to the Penobscot County jail and booked him."

"What happens now?"

"He'll hire an attorney either on his own or one will be provided for him, and they'll arraign him and set a trial date. After that it's a waiting game until the actual trial."

"It's all so senseless. He could probably have gotten away

with claiming self-defense with Howard Smith, but to have killed Sadie will be his downfall."

"That's true, but at least now Sadie's family will be able to have some peace knowing he's been caught and will face the consequences."

"Thank you so much for helping to make that happen. I know it had to be a leap of faith and a risk to your reputation to set up the meeting with the detectives based on how we got the confession and the glass."

Jim chuckled. "Don't give me too much credit. I was questioning my sanity nearly every step of the way and have to admit, I thought about backing out. It wasn't exactly kosher, but having that back up story saying you'd tricked him by pretending to have contacted Sadie made it a little easier, but I was grateful Phil and Dennis didn't push it. I think they were so happy to have at least something to go on, they were willing to let it slide. They could have saved face by saying it was one of those off-the-wall tips they get, but don't believe until it turns out to be true."

"Well, whatever swayed them to follow up, it was enough, and that's what counts."

"You've got that right."

"Why don't you come over tonight so we can celebrate? I'll get in touch with Jennifer and see if she'd like to join us."

"Sure. I'll even bring the champagne," Jim said.

CHAPTER THIRTY-SEVEN

*J*ennifer suggested inviting Annalise and Sarah as well. "They're just as much a part of this as we are," Jennifer told Eva.

It was a perfect June night when they all met at Eva's house. She had decided the best place to hold the celebration would be in the sunroom with the windows opened to let in the fresh air that felt so wonderful after a long winter. The combination of evergreen and hardwood trees that made up the woods surrounding the cleared area of her lawn provided a peaceful backdrop and the water feature in the herb garden enhanced the contented mood of the group. They were gathered in the cushioned patio chairs around a coffee table on which Eva had placed the charcuterie board she had prepared earlier that afternoon.

"It's so nice that you have this screened area," Sarah said with a small sigh, taking a slice of cheese and a cracker from the plate. "I don't think we would have survived out here with the black flies otherwise."

"To screened porches and captured killers," Annalise said, raising her glass in a toast.

"Hear, hear!" everyone else chimed in, raising their glasses for the toast.

"And to skeptics becoming believers," she added, holding up her glass in Jim's direction.

"To Jim," Jennifer joined in.

"To Jim," the three other Cozy Quilts Club members toasted as well.

Jim's face turned a shade of light pink but took the recognition in stride.

"I'm not sure I'm a hundred percent believer, but I've seen enough to keep my mind more open than it was before."

"It's a start," Eva said, smiling at him.

"One of us, one of us," Sarah chanted, which made everyone laugh, allowing Jim to get over his embarrassment.

"I got a call from Phil Roberts," Jennifer said. "He wanted to thank all of us for getting the confession from Stephen. They'd run out of leads, and he admitted they were afraid it was going to turn into a cold case. He definitely had his doubts, as did Dennis Smith, because of how we tricked Stephen into confessing. Apparently, when Stephen found out we had recorded his confession, he claimed he'd made it all up as a prank because he thought we were punking him. After they told him about the DNA matching the blood they found, he stopped talking and asked for his attorney."

"It sounds like Detective Roberts might be reconsidering that we'd made it up," Annalise said.

"That's what I thought, too. It wasn't anything he said directly, but something about his tone made me think he was hoping I would say more. There was enough doubt in his mind about it all being made up that he might actually believe we were telling the truth. He made a joke about having psychics to help solve cases in the future."

"Like I told Eva, stranger things have happened in investigations. Well, maybe not stranger than that," he conceded, and everyone laughed.

* * *

TWO HOURS LATER, they were still chatting amiably until Sarah glanced at her watch.

"Oh, my goodness! I had no idea we've been talking so long. I told Ashley I thought I would only be an hour. I'd better be getting home."

"Me, too," Jennifer said, glancing at her watch.

The party ended with everyone saying their goodbyes except Jim, who was staying the night.

"I like your friends," he told Eva.

"I'm glad. They're a pretty wonderful group and I think we're going to be even closer after this experience."

Nothing like solving a murder to bring a group together, Reuben said, looking up at Eva from where he sat on the kitchen floor.

She leaned down and gave him a scratch under his chin. "I'm so sorry. I wasn't thinking earlier. You deserve a special treat for your help in catching Stephen Hill," she said, taking a shrimp from the charcuterie board and placing it in his bowl.

Reuben's eyes opened wider, and he trotted over to the bowl, purring as he went.

"What do you think? Should we call it a night?" Eva asked Jim after putting away the food and placing the dishes in the dishwasher.

"You took the words right out of my mouth."

EPILOGUE

The next meeting of the Cozy Quilts Club was another celebration. Stephen Hill had been released on bail, but he would be going to trial for Sadie's and Howard's murders. As part of the terms of his release, he was placed on house arrest and would have to wear an ankle monitor.

"I can't thank you ladies enough," Jennifer said, tears in her eyes.

"It was a team effort," Annalise replied.

"This was one of those times when I was actually happy about being able to communicate with ghosts," Sarah said.

"Me, too," Eva agreed. "Both about you communicating with ghosts and me communicating with animals. And it wasn't just about solving Sadie's murder. I feel like a weight has been lifted now that Jim knows I have this ability. He may not be completely on board with accepting it, but my experiment with Reuben to convince him was something he couldn't argue with."

Reuben had walked into the sewing room at the mention of his name and was sitting beside Eva's chair.

"That was a brilliant idea, Reuben," Sarah exclaimed.

Reuben looked up at her and blinked his eyes in acknowledgement of the compliment.

It was, wasn't it?

Eva rolled her eyes. "It's outweighed only by your humility," she said sarcastically. "He had said, It was, wasn't it," she said for the benefit of the others.

They all laughed. In response, Reuben stood and walked haughtily back to the bay window and jumped up to his cushion, turning his back on them.

"Oh, no, I'm sorry, Reuben. I didn't mean to hurt your feelings by laughing," Jennifer said.

"He's fine. He needs to be taken down a peg every so often, otherwise he can be insufferable," Eva reassured her.

"Well, still. I am sorry, Reuben. You played a big part in this, too. I don't think I could have managed going to the police without Jim's support."

"I'm having a great time with the quilting part of our friendship, but I think I'm going to miss solving a murder. That was the first time I'd ever worked with someone else with paranormal abilities," Annalise said.

"I'd been thinking the same thing," Sarah said.

"Me, too," Eva said.

"Me, three… or is it four?" Jennifer asked, which brought a smile to everyone's face.

"I don't want there to be another murder, but who knows? Maybe there will be some other way we'll be able to do this again," Eva mused.

They all nodded their agreement, not knowing how prescient those words would be.

BOOK 2 EXCERPT

Prologue
Finding the Treasure
A Cozy Quilts Club Mystery

"Did you hear that?" Nellie Philpot turned from the kitchen sink where she was washing the dinner dishes to face her husband, Franklin "Frank" Philpot.

"All I can hear is wind, rain and thunder," he replied, his head buried in the daily newspaper.

As if to affirm his response, the dark sky lit with a bolt of lightning followed almost immediately with the boom of thunder, rattling the windows and making Nellie jump.

"Oh, my word! That sounds like it must be right over our heads!" she exclaimed. "I thought I heard a knock, but it must have been a tree branch brushing up against the house," she decided aloud and turned back to her dishes. As she did so another bolt of lightning lit the sky and briefly illuminated the view through the kitchen window over the sink and she let out a shriek and clapped her hand over her mouth as the image of a man appeared before her and almost as quickly disappeared.

Frank dropped the newspaper and looked up with concern on his face.

"What's the matter, Nellie?"

"I thought I saw a man outside," she said, her face pale. "I don't see him now, but I swear a face appeared right outside the window. It must have been my imagination, though. I can't see anyone now."

Letting out a grunt of annoyance, Franklin returned to his newspaper as a series of knocks sounded at the front door.

Nellie put her hand to her mouth again and her eyes grew round as she looked questioningly at Frank. He shrugged his shoulders in response to the unasked question of who was at the door.

"Stay here," he told her as he got up and walked to the front of the house where the knocking was emanating. "It must be a stranger in trouble. No one we know ever uses that door."

It might be a uniquely New England rural custom that the front door is rarely ever used and side entrances that most often enter into the kitchen are the preferred route of entry. If someone was at that door, it had to be a stranger and Frank approached cautiously. They lived in a rural area, with the nearest neighbor being half a mile away. He flicked on the switch for the porch light, and then pulled aside the curtain covering the sidelight to peer out onto the covered porch. He wanted to take a look at the visitor before opening the door but if someone was there, he was unable to see them. He was about to return to the kitchen thinking it must have been their imagination, as the only sounds were the howling wind, pouring rain and rumbling of thunder, not as close now, when there was another knock. He opened the door to find a man, his clothes drenched and clinging to him, leaning against the far side of the door as though he would fall down if he stood upright.

"Please help me. If he catches me, he'll shoot me again. He wants to kill me," he said as his body slid down and fell halfway through the open door.

"Nellie, bring some towels," Frank called out to her as he lifted the man under his arms and pulled him the rest of the way into the house. "And a blanket," he added before turning to close the door and bolt the lock. He gave another quick look out the sidelight, but the darkness and rain made it impossible to see if anyone else was outside. Whoever the man thought was after him was either hiding or not as close as he imagined.

Nellie bustled out of the kitchen. "Who is it, Frank? What's the matter?"

"He's passed out. He said someone's after him and trying to kill him. You go after the towels and blanket and I'll move him onto the couch in the living room."

She gave the man a quick look before passing by them and up the stairs to the linen closet. By the time she returned with them, Frank had dragged the still unconscious man into the living room and had removed his shoes, but he was still on the floor.

"Lay some towels down first. This guy is soaked to the bones. Why don't you put on the teakettle and I'll try to dry him off some before I do that. Maybe he'll wake up and be able to get himself up on the couch. A hot cup of tea might help him warm up."

Curious, but not wanting to be in the room while he dried the man off just in case he had to remove any of his clothing, Nellie returned to the kitchen and filled the teakettle and set it on the stove. She heard a soft moaning and then a cry of pain, and hurried back into the living room to find out what was happening. Frank had taken off the man's shirt and trousers, but he was still in his underclothes. The man had his arm around Frank's shoulder and Frank was supporting him around the waist as he lowered him onto the couch, where he had spread some towels.

179

Once the man was safely settled, he covered him with the blanket. They had been facing away from her when she'd entered the room, but as Frank was lowering him onto the couch, she saw the blotch of red on the man's undershirt that was obviously fresh blood.

"Oh, Frank! He's hurt."

"He's been shot," he replied, his mouth set. "You'll need to bring some bandages. Lots of them. As many as you can find."

Nellie ran from the room and up the stairs to their first aid supplies. Having a generous supply of bandages on hand was a necessity at a working farm and Nellie was glad she'd recently replenished their stock. Grabbing the basket with the gauze and tape, she hurried back down the stairs. Frank was lifting the undershirt as gently as possible, but the man let out a cry of pain when it pulled away from his skin where the bullet had entered. As Nellie laid the basket on the floor next to Frank, the whistling of the tea kettle alerted her it was ready.

"Don't put anything on the wound until I come back with the water. You'll need to wash away the blood first. It looks like it's not bleeding bad now, but you don't want it to get infected. I'll bring the iodine, too." She hurried back to the kitchen to take the angrily whistling kettle off the stove and was about to pour some into a bowl before changing her mind. Better to take the kettle with her and use one of the biggest mixing bowls. She grabbed clean dishcloths from the drawer and the bottle of iodine she kept on the window ledge above the sink and put them into the bowl so she could carry the kettle in her other hand. That wound was going to need a thorough washing. It seemed like she'd taken forever, but was only minutes until she reappeared in the living room to help Frank. He had retrieved the bottle of whiskey they kept for entertaining from the dining room and poured two fingers' worth into a glass which the man was drinking, grimacing either from pain or the whiskey. Nellie wasn't sure which.

"Thanks," he said between clenched teeth as he handed the empty glass back to Frank and then collapsed back onto the couch.

"I'm sorry. This is probably going to hurt but we need to get that wound cleaned and bandaged," Nellie told him as she put the supplies on the floor and lowered to her knees on the floor beside him. "Who did this to you?"

"Thanks. Just do what you need to do. I can take it," the man replied, but avoided answering her question.

She decided to let that go. "What's your name?" she asked instead, looking up at Frank in case he had already asked, but he shook his head.

"Frank. Frank Abbott."

"Well, what a coincidence. My husband's name is Frank, too," Nellie replied cheerily as she gently dabbed at the now dried blood farthest away from the hole in the man's side.

His body jerked as she got closer to the wound, but then stiffened and he clenched his teeth to hold back from crying out. She debated whether to keep talking and decided it might be best to try to take the man's mind off her ministrations.

"This has to be the worst storm we've had in years. I can't remember it raining this hard or the wind howling so much. Can you, Franklin?" She looked up at him and smiled.

He looked at her as though she'd gone mad and then realized what she was doing.

"No, can't say as I have. Can't imagine why anyone would be out on a night like this," he added. "What had you out, Frank?"

Frank's eyes had been tightly shut and the muscles in his jaw twitched from being clenched, but he opened them to look up at Franklin as though deciding whether to tell the truth. Franklin returned his gaze and remained quiet, but his demeanor told Frank that it wouldn't be wise to lie. He swallowed and took a deep breath to settle himself both for the pain and for what he was about to say.

"There are... were... three of us. We had a treasure map and were following the clues. Harvey had won it in a poker game. The guy who lost told him it had belonged to a pirate named Dixie Bull who was in Maine in the 1600s. We had two boats and were traveling up the Penobscot River and then to the Kenduskeag. John was in his copper bottom boat and Harvey and I were in the other one. We figured we'd need one just for the gold once we'd found it. Gold can be real heavy. A lot heavier than you'd think," he said by way of explanation for why they'd need an extra boat. "We each had a piece of the map so no one would pull a double-cross, but Harvey did anyway." His eyes turned hard. "Once we got to the spot where it looked like the gold would be buried and had pulled the boats up onto shore, he shot John and killed him. He would have killed me, too, but I was able to get a punch in and knocked him down and started running. That's when he shot me. The first one just grazed my arm, but he shot again and got me in my side. I didn't know where I was going, but just kept running until I thought I lost him. I didn't hear him coming after me, but then it got dark, and the storm came in. I'm lucky I found your house," he finished, his voice growing weaker as he spoke, and his eyes fluttered.

"You just rest now, Frank. The bleeding seems to have stopped, but you should probably stay still. Would you like a cup of tea? Something warm might help you feel better."

"No, thanks, ma'am. I think I'd just like to sleep awhile if that's okay with you."

"Of course. I'll get another blanket for you. You're starting to shiver," Nellie told him and looked at Franklin, who nodded in agreement, as she left the room. Once she returned and had tucked the quilt around Abbott, who had already fallen asleep, she and Franklin went into the kitchen out of earshot.

"The phone line must be down from the storm. I tried to call the sheriff while you were getting the quilt but couldn't raise the operator. I should go for the sheriff, but I don't want to leave you alone in case his partner... Harvey?" he asked, and Nellie nodded, "is still looking for him."

"Oh, yes, please don't leave me alone," Nellie said, her face showing her fear.

Franklin took her in his arms and held her close to reassure her.

"We'll just have to wait until morning and figure it out then. Maybe he will have his strength back after a good night's sleep and leave on his own. You go on to bed now. The doors are all locked and I have my hunting rifle and will stand guard."

She looked into his eyes, debating internally whether to argue, but she knew how stubborn he could be once he'd made up his mind to do something.

"Alright, I'll go to bed, but I'm not sure that I'll be able to sleep."

He smiled before telling her, "That's okay. You give it a try, anyway." He kissed the top of her head before releasing her from their embrace. "Go on now."

The night passed without incident and despite his best efforts, Franklin had dozed off in the chair he'd placed facing Frank Abbott, and with a line of sight toward the front door. As soon as he woke, he was aware something was wrong. He got up and walked over to the couch where Frank was still lying on his back and when he looked at his face, it was obvious he was dead but checked his pulse just to make sure. He pulled the quilt up over Frank's face so that Nellie wouldn't have to see and went to the kitchen to check the phone and the operator came on the line.

"Sally, this is Franklin Philpot. Would you tell the sheriff we need him to come to our house?"

"Sure, Franklin. Is something wrong?"

Knowing they were on a party line, and it was possible others were listening in, he avoided a direct answer. "Tell him it's no hurry, but we'll need to see him as soon as he's able to drop by," and then hung up.

He went into the dining room and gathered up Abbott's clothing, which Nellie had placed over the backs of the chairs to dry. In the pocket of Abbott's trousers, he found a wallet and inside was a folded piece of paper. He unfolded it and discovered it was what appeared to be a piece of a hand-drawn map. Abbott must have been telling the truth after all. Franklin tucked the paper into his own trousers as Nellie came down the stairs.

"Abbott is dead," he told her. "I've had Sally call the sheriff. We'll tell him what Abbott told us. I'm not sure it's going to help much since he didn't give us any full names other than his own and we don't know what direction he was coming from."

"But I thought he was just tired and needed rest last night," Nellie objected.

"He must have lost too much blood or gone into shock. He never woke up that I'm aware of."

Franklin took her arm and gently led her into the kitchen away from the body, where they both waited for the sheriff to arrive.

He never mentioned to her that he had taken the map and put it in the hidden compartment of the case that held his watch, tie clips, and cufflinks. But the story about the night Frank Abbott had shown up on their doorstep during one of the worst storms in decades, shot, and talking about buried gold and a copper bottom boat, was retold many times over the years and passed down through the generations.

ABOUT THE AUTHOR

After retiring from her day job of nearly 33 years, Marsha DeFilippo has embarked on a new career of writing books. She is also a quilter and lifelong avid crafter who has yet to try a craft she doesn't like. She spends her winters in Arizona and the remainder of the year in Maine.

For more information, please visit my website:
marsha defilippo.com

To get the latest information on new releases, excerpts and more, be sure to sign up for Marsha's newsletter.
https://marshadefilippo.com/newsletter

f facebook.com/Marsha-DeFilippo

X x.com/marshadefilippo

instagram.com/marshadefilippo

BB bookbub.com/authors/marsha-defilippo

pinterest.com/defilippo0699

a amazon.com/author/marshadefilippo

ALSO BY MARSHA DEFILIPPO

Arizona Dreams

Deja vu Dreams

Disillusioned Dreams

A Cozy Quilts Club Mystery series

Finding the Treasure

Summer's End

Caught in a Spider's Web

Counting Coins

Pulling Out the Hidden Stitches

(Click to download this free short story tie-in or use the QR code)

FREE BONUS MATERIAL

Receive your free copy of the Preview to *Follow the Crumbs*

Click here

Made in the USA
Monee, IL
15 February 2025